LOVE AND OTHER SPORTS

Short Stories and First Chapter Excerpts BANCROFT MYSTERIES

BANCROFT MYSTERIES COLLECTION

Murder By The Book

August Is Murder

Death Sting

Point of Murder

And the Band Played On

LOVE AND OTHER SPORTS

Bob Liter
Martie Liter Ogborn

Bancroft Mysteries, LLC

Copyright © 2020 Bob Liter and Martie L Ogborn

All rights reserved. The characters and events portrayed in this book are fictitious. Any similarity to real persons, living or dead, is coincidental and not intended by the author.

No part of this book may be reproduced, stored in a retrieval system, or transmitted in any form or by any means, electronic, mechanical, photocopying, recording, or otherwise, without express written permission of the publisher.

First published in 2020 by Independent Publisher
Second Edition (Enhanced: new supplementary material) published in 2023

By Bancroft Mysteries, LLC
Mackinaw, IL 61755
www.BancroftMysteries.com
ISBN 978-1-958521-12-0 (eBook)
ISBN 978-1-958521-00-7 (Paperback)
Printed in the United States of America

CONTENTS

Title Page
BANCROFT MYSTERIES COLLECTION
Title Page
Copyright
THE GIRL NEXT DOOR	1
THE SPELLING BEE	5
BRUCE	13
SMOKE CLOUDED MY GUILT	23
MY SISTER'S WEDDING	34
THE RESCUE	38
PRESSURE POINT	42
TUMBLEWEED AND GOOSEBERRY PIE	47
THE WAITRESS	50
NOW I'M TALKING	55
IMPRESSING MARY LOW	59
BONUS BABY	65
HOUSEKEEPING 101	71
THE SNOWSTORM	76
THE WAY THE COOKIE CRUMBLES	79
ELEMENTARY	83

THE CON GAME	87
THE ROOT OF THE MATTER	91
NOW I GET IT	98
MY FAVORITE SPEECH	108
WHAT WAS HE THINKING?	112
THANKSGIVING WITH THE BANCROFT'S	115
WHERE ARE THEY NOW?	118
MURDER BY THE BOOK - CHAPTER ONE	121
AUGUST IS MURDER - CHAPTER ONE	130
DEATH STING - CHAPTER ONE	133
A POINT OF MURDER - CHAPTER ONE	137
AND THE BAND PLAYED ON - CHAPTER ONE	141
MURDER INHERITED - CHAPTER ONE	147
Acknowledgements	151
NOTE FROM THE PUBLISHER	153
Books By This Author	155
ABOUT THE AUTHORS	159

THE GIRL NEXT DOOR
By **BOB LITER**

I came home to an empty house the day I returned from my freshman year at State College. Dad was driving a load of cattle feed across Kansas, and Mother was working at Crestwood Community Bank downtown. I'd have stopped there, but it was nearly four o'clock, and she'd be home soon.

I glanced apprehensively at the house to the east where Mandy Anders lives. I hoped she wouldn't come running out to pester me. I did look forward to seeing her again. But that could wait. I hoped she wouldn't still be making me feel like a worm with those big brown eyes because I didn't take her to the high school prom the spring before. I was a senior, of course, and she was only a junior. Who wants to go to a prom with his sister? She's not really my sister, but she might as well have been the way she tagged after me.

I glanced at the house to the west where Beth Ann Crosley lives. She was voted queen of our high school class. She had always been a queen as far as I was concerned.

She let me do her homework, wash her red convertible, and do any other chores she was above doing, but she wouldn't go to the prom with me. She went with Gary Showalter, the star quarterback, the lead in two school plays, and a guy with muscles, dark hair, and a smile for everyone, even me. I hated him then but realized later that he was a nice guy.

I thought of all this as I stepped out of my tired Honda and stretched. Was Beth Ann still dating Gary? I sighed, popped the back end of the Honda, and gathered my dirty clothes. I shoved them into the washing machine in the house and plopped down on the living room couch. I was asleep when Mom got home. She hugged me, scolded me for not sorting my clothes before I put them in the washer, and praised me for not failing any of my college courses.

Dinner appeared on the kitchen table while I washed up. We ate and talked. Home cooking. It was great. Dad called at seven and told us he'd complete his run the next day and be home after that. I went to bed and slept until ten the following day.

I took my time getting up, enjoyed a slow, hot shower, and put on clean jeans, a T-shirt that smelled fresh, and sandals. I made the bed, proving I'd learned something at college.

In the kitchen, I lingered over coffee and read Mom's note, "Ron, if you have time, please mow the grass. Your father will be tired when he gets home."

And so I was directing the mower toward Mandy's house when Beth Ann tapped on my shoulder, hugged me when I turned off the mower, and gave me a smile warmer than any I remembered from her in the past. She'd never hugged me before.

"Welcome home. Great to see you."

"Beth Ann. Great to see you. How's Gary?"

"Gary, who? Showalter? That scum. I have nothing, absolutely nothing to do with him. He married Flossie Cramer not long after you left for college. Let's talk about something, someone else. She's already pregnant. How did you like college? You didn't flunk, did you? Want to come over to my house? We could listen to some records or something. Nobody's home."

I leaned against the mower. I had hoped Beth Ann would pay attention to me like she did Gary in the past. And now?... I surprised myself when I said, "Maybe tomorrow. I need to finish mowing the yard."

Beth Ann's eyes widened. She seemed as surprised as I was when I turned down a chance to be with her. She stuck her nose

in the air, turned, and walked back to her house. I watched her hips sway and smacked my forehead with the heel of my hand.

Was I out of my mind? Before I had time to answer myself, I heard a door slam and Mandy's voice.

"Hi, big man on campus," she shouted.

She skipped across the grass. This was Mandy? She wore blue jeans as usual, but they were pressed and fit her legs like a second skin. Her chest filled out the white blouse in a rounded way I didn't remember. And her hair. Each strand was as independent as ever but shorter with colorful highlights. It was still sandy, but there were dark strands here and there. Her eyes sparkled. That hadn't changed. But her lips seemed fuller, more inviting. The little girl who had followed me around, the girl who pouted only last year because I wouldn't take her to a high school dance, had become a knockout.

Hello, Mandy," I said with wonder in my voice.

She smiled. No, she did more than that. She grinned like her ship had come in or something. We talked about college and how she would go to one in the next state come fall. I forgot about Beth Ann and lost all desire to date her. It was Mandy. She skipped onto her family's mailbox on the curb, gathered catalogs and letters, waved to me, and disappeared into her house.

I waited an hour before I knocked on her front door. She opened it eventually and stood with a cell phone against her ear.

"Okay, Robbie, I'll see you tonight," she said and shut the phone. Offered me lemonade. We sat on the patio in the back. She had changed to shorts and a T-shirt that clung gratefully to her bosom. I talked around it for a while but finally had to ask, "Who's Robbie?"

"He's my fiancé," she cooed.

"Aren't you? I mean, I always thought of you as so young. Too young to be engaged."

"I'm only a year younger than you, Mr. College Man."

Later, as I sat in the kitchen waiting for Mom to get home and fix supper, I realized I felt good about Mandy's evident happiness and that I didn't like Beth Ann. I got the high school yearbook out and decided to call Charlene Chatsworth. She wasn't home.

THE SPELLING BEE
By **BOB LITER**

I was a disgrace the day Millie Crawford, me, and two boys represented Woodrow Wilson in the regional spelling bee at Collingsworth High in Springfield. The boys wore blue jeans and clean running shoes. All the girls from the various schools except me had their hair combed, their makeup on, and wore dresses and dress shoes.

Millie's mother picked me up an hour earlier than I expected because she had to run an errand for her boss at Heartland Insurance Company. I pulled my hair back from my face and secured it with a rubber band. My face was bare of makeup, and I wore faded blue jeans and raunchy running shoes.

Once there, we killed time until a beautiful young man appeared on the auditorium stage, fussed with the microphone, and placed eight folding chairs in a row.

"Oh," Millie said, "That's the radio disc jockey who plays that cool stuff. He's on television on weekends. Does the weather. Mike Shane, that's his name."

"Spellers, please take your places here on the stage," Mike Shane said.

We paraded to the chairs. He smiled at me. I sat down and tried not to stare at him.

"Robert Ward," Mike Shane said in a clear, intimate voice. Robert, a tall guy with a butch haircut, marched to the center of the stage.

"Your word is intangible."

"Intangible." Mike Shane pronounced it again, loud and clear. Robert Ward spelled the word correctly without hesitation.

I fidgeted, released my hair, fluffed it out so it came down to my shoulders, and waited as each of the other spellers got through their first word.

"Elizabeth Jones," Mike Shane said. I sat there for a moment, still dazzled by his smile. He had said my name. I rose and moved to the center of the stage.

He looked directly into my eyes, smiled, and said, "The word for you is alluring."

He pronounced it again, slowly.

My mind finally engaged.

"Alluring," I said. "A-l-l-u-r-i-n-g."

It seemed a lifetime before he said, "Correct."

When we were down to four competitors and were on a ten-minute break, Millie said, "Gosh, Liz, I thought you would be eliminated on that first word. What happened?"

"It was as though he was telling me I was alluring. Isn't that ridiculous? Me, plain Liz, alluring? Still, it seemed like that's what he was saying."

"Yeah, you wish. He was telling you what word you should spell."

"I know, I know," I sighed.

Millie and I both lost in the next round. I misspelled accelerator by spelling it "acceleratEr." We were disappointed, of course, but we stayed until the end. Robert Ward won by spelling "thermoelement."

I listened to Mike Shane's radio show at home and watched him on television. Millie was there the following Saturday, waiting to go to a movie with me.

"If we don't leave soon, we'll miss half the show," Millie said as I sat in front of our living room TV.

"We'll get there in time," I insisted. "It's only a movie."

"Have your parents noticed how interested in weekend

weather you are all of a sudden?"

"Don't you dare tell 'em," I said. "I know it's silly, but he's so handsome and has the nicest smile."

While Millie and I were at the movie, Mike Shane telephoned my house.

"Who is this Mike Shane who called last night?" Dad demanded the next morning.

"Mike Shane called me?"

"That's what he called himself. Said he was coming up from Springfield to get permission to date you."

"To date me?"

"That's what he said. Who is this guy, anyway?"

"When did he say he'd be here?"

"Sometime this evening, I think," Dad said.

Mother fixed my hair, and we decided on my blue dress. Dad let me get a new pair of shoes, and Mother had a cute little matching box purse.

Mike arrived at our house, the one with the porch that needed painting, the one with the broken front step, the one with the worn living room carpet, and the one with the dining room table that had more dents than my Dad's Ford pickup.

Mike looked like something out of a men's magazine. A beige sportcoat rested on his broad shoulders, contrasting with a dark brown shirt open at the throat. His slacks matched the shirt, and his shoes were soft leather loafers.

"May I come in," he said.

"Oh, sorry, of course," I said.

He shook Dad's hand and said something to Mother that made her eyes shine.

"I'm here to ask permission to take Elizabeth to dinner and a movie. If you approve? And if she wants to."

"Liz, aren't you going to say anything?" Mother asked.

I managed to draw my eyes away from Mike's and said, "Yes."

Dad said, "Lizzy doesn't appear to know much about you. How did you two meet?"

Mike folded his hands in his lap.

7

"My father is a physician in Springfield. My mother is an attorney. I'm about to finish college with a journalism degree. I've worked as a radio disk jockey and a part-time television weatherman. We met at the spelling bee. I was the announcer."

Finally, the questions were over. Mike promised to have me back by eleven. A maroon convertible with the top down was parked in front of our house. My parents stood on the porch. Dad said, "Look at that car; just look at that."

We were out of town in no time and breezing down Interstate 55 toward Springfield.

"I thought we'd stop at Carletta's and have dinner before we go to the movie. We have plenty of time."

Carletta's was one of those places you took people to impress them.

"Why me?" I asked.

I'd been trying to get up my nerve enough to ask the question for the last five minutes.

"I'm twenty-three years old, thinking about settling down, and I fell in love with you at the spelling bee. I can't explain it. You're different, so maybe I shouldn't say it."

"What?"

"Well, I never saw any woman look sexier than you did with your hair so wild and free. Your image followed me around like a happy cloud."

He called me a woman and sexy. I knew what he meant by falling in love so quickly. I'd done the same thing. What if he changed his mind after he got to know me? The food and service were excellent. The waitress called him Mr. Shane. He charged the meal on a credit card, and the waitress thanked him for what must have been a generous tip.

The movie? Harrison Ford was in it. And somewhere after the first few minutes, Mike held my hand. He kissed me on the porch after bringing me home at ten minutes to eleven.

"I'll call you," he said as he waved goodbye from the side of his car. Was I dreaming? I looked around to make sure it was my house.

Saturday, we went on a picnic. It was raining when we got to an isolated grassy area beside a small stream a few miles from town. Tall elm and oak trees formed a canopy over the grass, but eventually, rain dripped through the foliage.

We sat on a blanket, ate sandwiches, and drank champagne. It tickled my nose. He said, "Close your eyes." I did. He took my left hand and slid a ring on my finger.

"Look," he said. I looked. The stone in the ring -- I remember thinking it had to be an imitation because it was so big -- sparkled as rain fell on it.

"Will you marry me," he said, his voice firm, his eyes gazing into mine. They were blue, sometimes with a hint of green in them.

"Please say yes," he said. He got up on his knees and put his hands together as if in prayer.

"Yes," I said.

Later, when his kisses had utterly disarmed me, we struggled out of our wet clothes. I hid the ring when I got home, but that night, when I saw Millie, I wore it.

"I'm engaged to Mike Shane."

"My God, Liz, are you really? After two dates? What a rock. Is it real?"

"I don't know," I said. "Maybe."

Three days later, I hadn't heard from Mike. I spent a lot of time in my room thinking about what I'd done and wondering if I'd ever see him again. He appeared at my house on the fourth day, right at supper time. Dad was annoyed, but Mother urged him to join us. He said he'd just eaten.

"I've got something important to discuss. Take your time, please. I'll wait in the living room."

Between bites of meatloaf and potatoes, Dad said, "Something important to discuss with us?" He glared at me.

At last, the meal was finished. Mother didn't even clear off the table. We paraded into the living room. I sat on the couch beside Mike. Mother sat across from us in her knitting chair, and Dad sat in his recliner.

Mike took my hand and held my ring finger. After a questioning look, he took a deep breath and said, "I've asked Liz to marry me. I gave her a ring, but she isn't wearing it. I don't understand."

"I've got it right here," I said. It was attached to a silver chain I wore around my neck. I pulled it from under my blouse.

Dad said I was too young. Mother smiled. Mike said he would have a full-time job at the station when he got his degree and hoped we could get married then. After many questions and discussions, it was agreed that I could marry him.

The wedding was a mother's dream: wedding gown, garter, brides' maids, all the trimmings in a huge Springfield church. We met Mike's parents, of course, and lots of his friends, including young women. Finally, all the innuendos, the toasts, the dancing, and the drinking ended. Mike and I slipped away while the partying continued.

Our wedding night was so fabulous I won't even try to describe it. We started our married life in Mike's four-room apartment. The days flew by. Morning sickness and the growing size of my stomach were unpleasant. Still, Mike was considerate and complimented me on how my face had taken on an angelic glow.

One day Mike's father visited while Mike was at work and said, "This place looks better than the last time I saw it. Mike never learned to pick up his clothes."

"I know," I said.

"I'll get to the point. Got to get to the hospital. I've started a bank account in your name." He handed me a black bank book.

"Mike has no fiscal responsibility. There's four thousand dollars in the account. You'll have to use three thousand to pay off his credit cards. They still come to our house." He handed me five credit-card bills. "Just pay them off without saying anything to him. I'll add a thousand dollars to your account each month. You manage the money. There's no sense in my keeping the money until I die. I'll talk Mike into getting rid of those damned credit cards."

A few days after, I cleaned the apartment, washed the dishes, and did the laundry. I was folding clothes on the kitchen table when I started crying. The thought of taking care of a baby and Mike overwhelmed me. I was so tired. I was in bed when Mike's "Liz, where are you?" woke me. He came into the room and sat beside me.

"Do you know what day it is?" he asked. His eyes glistened.

"Thursday, isn't it?"

"It's May 28."

I sat up and rubbed my eyes. May 28th?

"The day we met. The word for you is beautiful," he said.

"Oh, I'll bet."

"Spell your word, please, Miss."

"B-e-a-u-t-i-f-u-l."

"Congratulations. You are this year's spelling bee winner."

"What's the prize?" I asked.

He opened a small, black jewelry box and displayed diamond earrings.

"These are for you to wear tonight when I take you to dinner at Carletta's," he said.

The years rolled by. He remembered every time. The fourth year, after I had thrown a fit when he bought a new convertible, my spelling word was "frugal." I spelled it and pouted.

"I know you expected something better than frugal," he said. "I made a mistake. That wasn't your word; the word for you is sensual."

I spelled it and said, "At least that's more romantic."

"And because you're so sensual, so beautiful, so loving, so so, I . . . well here."

He handed me the keys to the convertible. I tried to give them back, but he wouldn't take them. I retrieved my purse from the kitchen table and handed him the keys to our ten-year-old Chevy sedan. We laughed and hugged each other.

My small two-ring binder eventually had twenty-one cards, my spelling word for each year.

That last year Mike sat beside my bed in the hospital after our daughter had left to get some sleep. I shuddered about how I looked; I'd lost all my hair because of the chemo.

Mike said, "I know you're not asleep."

I opened my eyes and said, "You don't know what day it is, do you?"

"Wednesday, isn't it?"

"It's the anniversary of the day we met," I said, "and the word for me is grateful. G-R-A-T-E-F-U-L."

BRUCE
By **BOB LITER**

Clark Farnsworth sat on the edge of the bed, stretched his long naked body, and snatched up the phone. He dialed the Hemstead Apartments' super.

"Yeah, what is it?"

"He's barking again, Harry. I can't sleep. Do something about it, or I'll break in and kill the damned dog."

Clark imagined Harry sitting on his ass in his basement domain, sucking on a beer.

"I'll talk to her again, Mr. Farnsworth. Having the dog is included in her lease. It's so little I didn't think it would be a problem."

"Her curves and those big blues have anything to do with it, Harry? I've seen the way you look at her."

"Maybe you look at her the same way, Mr. Farnsworth. I hope you can get some sleep. I'll talk to her."

"You do that. In the meantime, I'm recording that dog's yapping. You'd think it would get tired eventually and shut up."

Clark hung up the phone and placed the recorder on a chair near the wall between his apartment and the yapping dog. He tapped on the wall. The dog resumed barking. He sat in front of the computer in the living room. He typed, "The trouble with you, Hobart, is you don't have any balls."

"You know that's not true, Virginia. You've had your eager

little hands on them often enough."

Clark sat back, pressed his hands over his ears, got up, and went to the kitchen. He warmed leftover coffee. Back in his chair, he listened to the dog yap and stared at the screen.

As was often his custom when he wasn't sure about the dialog he had written, he read it aloud. Was the bit about Hobart not having any balls too strong? Was it something Virginia would say? What about the name Hobart? Was it suitable for the character?

Clark stood, paced around the room, grabbed the coffee cup, and took it to the kitchen. He returned to the bed, squashed a pillow around his head, and tried to block out the barking. He did sleep. Not much and surely not enough. He got up, pushed his legs into jeans he picked up from the edge of the bed, and stretched. The radio clock on the nightstand read seven a.m.

"You can't sleep, so sit your ass down and write," he said aloud.

He had to finish his Cynthia Castle romance or stop eating. He stared at the screen and listened to his stomach growl. He stood, walked to the kitchen, looked in the refrigerator, smelled something terrible, found some green apple sauce, threw it out, and finished dressing.

He turned on his cassette player and filled the apartment with the sounds of a trio playing the old standards. After listening for a minute, he left the apartment and paced in front of the elevator door, waiting for it to come up from the lobby.

Clark frowned at the woman who came out of the elevator and watched her hips sway as she went to the apartment next to his and unlocked the door. A dog about the size of a weasel bounced around under the woman's feet. Clark was treated to a display of bare thighs as she leaned over and picked up the dog.

She turned away from him and started to enter the apartment.

"Ah, Miss, may I speak to you for a moment?"

"What is it?"

It's about your dog. It barks all day. It keeps me awake."

She hitched the wiggling dog up against her chest and said, "You sleep all day?"

"I work nights."

"Oh, what do you do?"

"It doesn't matter what I do; that damned dog interferes with my sleep."

"Hear that, Poops? You've got to stop barking."

She started to enter the apartment again.

"I made a recording. Want to hear what Poops sounds like while I'm trying to sleep?"

Clark motioned toward his open door.

"No thanks. If you have any complaints, file them with the super."

"I already have," Clark said. "I'll get the tape, and you can listen to it in your apartment."

He entered his apartment, returned with the recording, and was pleased to see she was still waiting.

"What's that music you're playing? Rather loud, I might add."

Clark held the tape out toward her and drew it back as Poops snapped at his fingers.

"The music? Beegie Adair Trio. Why?"

"It's a nice sound. I like those oldies."

She held Poops to the side, reached out, and took the tape.

He left the building, walked the block and a half to Carson's Café, and ate eggs, toast, and apple pie alamode.

He finished and drummed his fingers on the table. She seemed reasonable, he thought as he imagined the young woman listening to the tape.

"That was fast," the waitress, Emmy, said as Clark motioned for the bill.

"Yeah, I guess. Got to get back."

He left his usual tip and hurried back to Hemstead Arms. He hesitated after getting off the elevator and knocked on her door. She opened it without releasing the chain, peeked out, and said, "Oh, it's you."

She slammed the door, came back in an instant, opened the door, and threw the tape out the small opening. She slammed the door again. Clark picked up the tape and felt blood rush to his face. Damn her. He rapped on the door again and again.

The elevator door groaned open, and Ms. Morganthal, floppy hat and all, stepped out. She headed for her apartment down the hall. Clark rapped on the door again.

Ms. Morganthal turned, put a gloved hand to her face, and said, "I've been meaning to talk to you about that music. You play it too loud sometimes and too late."

"Oh," he said. "Sorry about that. I'll watch it."

Clark reached to pound on the apartment door again just as it opened.

"Yes, he does, Ms. Morganthal. I agree," the young woman in the doorway said.

Poops raced between the woman's legs and wagged its tail so hard its rump swung back and forth. Clark scooped up the dog and handed it to the woman.

"Okay, you're right about the music. I'll watch it. Why did you throw the tape at me?"

"It's obscene. You ought to be ashamed of yourself."

"Obscene?"

Clark pointed the tape at her and said, "What's obscene is the way that weasel barks. It doesn't even sound like a real dog."

"Goodnight, Martha; you and I will have to talk to the super about this," said Ms. Morganthal.

Ms. Morganthal entered her apartment and closed the door with a bang.

So, Martha was the dog owner's name.

There must be a civilized way to resolve this, Clark thought.

Martha closed her apartment door quietly. Clark entered his apartment and turned the music down. He sat at his computer and listened to a slow rendition of Love Me Forever.

It was no good at first. He kept thinking of Martha. Mattie, he would call her. He realized the dog wasn't barking. He typed out a fictionalized version of what had just happened in the hallway. He soon was turning out pages of a new Cynthia Castle romance. He liked it. Had conflict, emotion -- he'd have to expand the plot -- an attractive protagonist. Yes, Mattie was a beauty. Nice shape, gorgeous hair, and those eyes. He wrote for three hours solid. And then he hit the sack, for once able to sleep during the day.

Now his schedule was really screwed up. And what a name for a dog. He had a dog once. Named it Bruce after a favorite cartoon character.

He put the tape in the player to get to the end of yesterday's recording so he could resume recording the barking. He was in the kitchen looking for something to eat when he heard his voice saying something about one of his fictional characters having her hands around a man's balls. He adjusted the tape and heard himself reading dialog from his earlier writing. No wonder Mattie was pissed.

He leaned against the outside of his apartment door for fifteen minutes before she came out.

"On your way to work?" he asked.

"Breakfast. Don't have to be at work until nine."

"May I join you?"

"No."

"I want to apologize for what was on that tape."

She headed for the elevator.

"You should," she said over her shoulder.

"I will, at breakfast."

She turned. "You can apologize now, although I can't imagine how you could justify what you said on that tape."

The elevator arrived. She got in and tried to get out when he entered. The door closed. She did not try to stop it.

"I'm a writer," Clark said.

"Of course you are," Mattie said as she backed into a corner.

She hurried out as he stood away from the opened elevator door on the first floor. Clark lengthened his stride to keep up. A block later, she ducked into Carson's Café and sat in a booth near the front.

"Hi, Clark," Emmy, the waitress, said as Clark sat across from Mattie.

"Emmy, this is Mattie," Clark said.

"I know," the waitress said. "What will it be this morning?"

"Orange juice, coffee, and the usual bagel," Mattie said.

"You eat here regularly?" Mattie asked. "I never noticed you before."

"Don't usually get here this early," Clark said.

"So, you claim to be a writer."

"That's what I claim. I write romances," Clark said.

"C'mon. A rugged guy like you writes romances?"

"Yeah. I write a Western now and then. I tried mysteries but was no good at that. There's a demand for romances. So, I write them."

Emmy placed a tray in the empty booth next to them and set Mattie's breakfast in front of her.

She put eggs, toast, and apple pie alamode in front of Clark.

Mattie gazed at the pie and ice cream. Clark waited for her to say something. She shook her head, drank orange juice, and watched Clark gobble eggs and toast. He took a deep breath and started on the pie and ice cream.

"You must be in a hurry," Mattie said.

"Not really. Just habit. When I worked at the Gazette, I had half an hour for lunch—been eating too fast ever since.

"Now you sleep all day and write romances at night," Mattie said.

"Yeah, it's crazy, I guess. I was still working at the paper during the day when I started writing fiction at night. Now it seems it's the only time I can write."

Mattie wiped her mouth with a paper napkin, placed it on her plate, and stood.

"You notice the dog doesn't bark when you're home?" Clark asked.

"Yes, I wonder if that recording of yours is faked somehow. However, it does sound like Poops.

"The dog is lonely, maybe scared when you're gone. That's why it barks."

"How would you know that?"

"Just read it somewhere, I guess."

"Maybe you should sit with it while I'm gone. Then it wouldn't bark, and you could write your romances."

"Oh no, I'm not babysitting your dog."

Mattie turned to go.

Clark pictured himself talking to Mattie every morning as she left the dog with him.

Wait a minute," he said. "I guess I could try it for a day or so. I've got to get some writing done."

"You won't be mean to Poops, will you?"

The next morning as he was about to go to bed, a knock on the door stopped him. He threw a bathrobe over his shoulders and opened the door. Mattie stood there with Poops in her arms.

Clark stared.

"You said you wanted to keep Poops in the daytime so she wouldn't be lonely and stop barking."

"I did say that, didn't I? Okay, could you give me the dog? As he reached out for it, his bathrobe threatened to open. He held it closed with one hand and held the dog in the other."

She said, "Don't bite him now, Poops," and was gone.

Clark stood by the door holding the wiggling dog. He sat it down and watched as it explored the apartment. Dogs leave doo-doo behind. Oh well, he'd worry about that later. He'd been pounding on the computer keys all night and was tired. He threw the bathrobe on a chair beside the bed and crawled in. He was almost asleep when the dog bounced from the floor onto the bed and next to him. He looked into begging dark eyes the size of little marbles as the dog bounded up and down.

He reached over, caught the dog on the upswing, put it at the foot of the bed, and went to sleep. Several hours later, he was up making coffee. A knock on his door made him realize he anticipated seeing Mattie when she came to pick up her dog. He smiled as he opened the door.

"Had the best sleep I've had in weeks," Clark said, predicting her question.

"Poops didn't keep you awake then. What did she do all day?"

"For one thing, she peed on my kitchen floor. Guess I'll have to take her for a walk in the morning."

"Well, I guess this might work out then."

"Seems so."

"I've got a date this Saturday night. Maybe you'd take care of her then."

"Maybe," Clark said.

Mattie stooped, picked up Poops, and said, "Well, thanks. I'll let you get to work. I'd like to read one of your books. I looked for them in the library during my lunch hour."

"My pen name is Cynthia Castle. They wouldn't be under my real name. How did you know my name anyway?"

Ms. Morganthal must have mentioned it.

"Cynthia Castle. Really! Are you telling me Cynthia Castle is a man? YOU are Cynthia Castle! THE Cynthia Castle!"

"Yeah, that's me. Are you one of my readers?"

"That stuff is too lurid for me."

"Life is lurid," Clark said.

"Poops," he said when he was alone with the dog the following day, "that's no name for a dog. Let's take off that silly pink ribbon around your neck. Here's something for you."

Clark stooped and fastened a miniature, spiked, studded dog collar around Poops' neck. The fake spikes glistened.

Clark said, "There. Now you look like a dog. And I'm going to call you Bruce. Maybe the collar and the name will show the other dogs in the park you're nobody to fool with.

Bruce stopped at an evergreen tree along the way, sniffed, and left her mark. In the park, she pooped and ran around and around, apparently chasing an unseen rabbit. A woman with a police dog on a chain appeared. The dog strained to get at Bruce. Clark picked the little dog up and carried it to his apartment.

He dumped a can of dog food Mattie had left into a bowl, put fresh water in another bowl, and sat down. Eventually, he fixed himself a couple of eggs and toast. By the time he finished eating, the dog was asleep on the kitchen floor. He tiptoed into the bedroom, shed his clothes, and slept until a knock roused him.

Mattie stood outside.

"Come in," Clark said. "Bruce."

The dog raced to the door, its claws sliding on the floor. Mattie picked it up and said, "Bruce?"

"That's her name now. The collar lets the dogs at the park know she's nobody to fool with."

"You took her to the park? I was always afraid one of those big dogs would hurt her. And what's that thing around her neck?"

"It's not as heavy as it looks. If you were another dog, would you fool with one named Bruce who wears a collar like that?"

Mattie laughed, a musical sound that tingled in the air long after she left.

"I've read "Return of Love" and started "Lost Love." Enjoyed the humor, but not so keen about those lurid love scenes."

"Well, that's what sells books. Human males and females do that stuff, you know."

"So I've heard," Mattie said. "She cuddled the dog in her arms, stepped out in the hall, and said, "Bruce." The dog wagged its tail.

***

"It's a lonely old town," Clark said Saturday night as he and Bruce sat on the living room couch. Clark read, and Bruce pushed her nose against his leg.

"How was the date?" Clark asked when Mattie returned at 10 p.m. carrying a pale blue paper sack.

"Nothing special," Mattie said as she sat on the couch and scratched behind one of the dog's ears."

Clark scratched the other ear as the dog sprawled between them.

Mattie fished a pink leash out of the sack.

"Bruce sniffed, raised her nose, and jumped off the couch.

"She doesn't like it. Doesn't fit her image as a fierce fighting dog," Clark said.

"How do you know all those details you put in your novels?"

"Just imagination. That's what fiction writing is. Using your imagination."

"Are you sure that couch love scene you seem to write into every novel isn't more than imagination?"

"It does seem real by now," Clark said as his arm glided around Mattie's shoulder.

"Is this the part where the girl turns and bats her big blues at the hero's face?"

"Right. Then the guy takes the girl's face in his hands and kisses her on the lips."

They held their positions until Mattie moved her face out of Clark's hands and maneuvered her neck.

"I don't remember writing that into one of those scenes," Clark said.

Mattie rubbed her neck, picked up Clark's hands, and placed them on her face.

She noticed that Clark's eyes, only inches from hers, were dreamy green, or were they blue-green.

"If you don't kiss me, my neck will get stiff again."

Clark kissed her warm, moist lips. They moved against his. His tongue explored. Mattie's shoes thudded onto the floor. Bruce jumped down and sat looking up at Mattie and Clark. The dog jumped out of the way when they tumbled to the floor. They began clawing at each other's clothes.

Bruce strolled to the corner of the room, curled up, and went to sleep.

SMOKE CLOUDED MY GUILT
By **BOB LITER**

"You are a genuine bitch," Tom Swanson said as I was getting ready to leave the insurance office.

Then, much to my surprise, he added, "How about you and me going to dinner tonight?"

"If I'm such a bitch, why would you want to take me to dinner?" I snapped as I locked the central drawer to my desk and started to get up to leave.

He stretched his long frame onto my desk, and as he sat there, his outstretched hand held me gently in my chair. He was smiling at me, and his blue eyes sparkled as they always did whenever we were engaged in verbal combat. I brushed his hand aside, but I stayed in the chair.

"It's because you're such a bitch that I want to have dinner with you. We've been at each other's throats for weeks. Don't you think it would be more pleasant around here if we had a long talk and tried to iron out our differences?

It would be nice to have dinner with someone, I was thinking. I was about to tell him for the hundredth time to not sit on my desk when he said, "I promise to take you to the non-smoking section of the restaurant, and, of course, I promise not to smoke." Our spatting had started over his pipe and the billowing smoke he created every time he lit the thing.

The first six months I worked there after my husband died, I had put up with it because I needed the job and was grateful to have the chance to learn. Tom was the star salesman of the staff, and even though I hated the smoke with a passion, I put up with it.

"Well, I do have to eat," I said as I got up from the chair, "and if you're not going to smoke, all right, but I'm going to pay my share.

He slid off the desk, and we walked outside into a warm summer evening. I had no idea it would be anything more than two single people having dinner together.

"There's a restaurant only a couple of blocks from here. I've always thought the food was OK. "Let's walk," he said.

"The food is fine. I've eaten there often," I replied.

As we walked along briskly, he began stuffing tobacco into his pipe. I was almost breathless as I said, "Slow down a little.

My legs aren't as long as yours. And I thought you were not going to smoke."

"I won't smoke while we eat; that's all I promised. Surely there's enough fresh air out here for you to breathe. Besides, the breeze will blow it away from you. I made sure of that before I even considered smoking." He said the last with exaggerated sarcasm in his voice.

Am I a genuine bitch? I wondered as we walked at a reasonable pace to the restaurant. I knew I disliked myself each morning when I looked in the mirror. My looks hadn't changed since my husband died. I still had the same reddish-brown hair, the same slightly too-large nose, and the small mouth that seemed to be turned down all the time. I didn't know what I disliked about myself, but now I always felt uneasy as I looked in the mirror.

My husband's death after a heart attack turned me into a vocal opponent of smoking. I hated breathing someone else's smoke and never smoked myself. I hated everything about smoking, and I'm afraid I was even beginning to hate people who smoke.

We ordered drinks and dinner, and then Tom said, "Boy, it sure is pleasant sitting here in all this clean air of the non-smoking section. I feel healthier already."

The man could make me furious! He had almost cost me my job only a couple of weeks earlier when I complained about his smoking. He was sitting with his feet on his desk, puffing away at his pipe and purposely blowing the stuff in my direction.

I just couldn't take it anymore, even though Tom was in the office only an hour or so a day and sometimes not at all.

I jumped up from my chair and marched into Mr. Jones's office without knocking. He is the boss and owner of the insurance agency. I demanded that he do something about Tom Swanson's smoking.

"He's doing it on purpose, just to spite me because I complained about it when none of the other girls had the nerve," I hissed as I tried to keep my voice under control.

The "other girls" were two older women working in the office. I called them red and white to myself. One had outlandishly dyed red hair, and the other's was as white as a cloud.

Mr. Jones' kind, round face sagged as he sighed and said, "Damn that Tom. He's the best insurance salesman I've ever had but loves to stir up trouble. Ask him to come in here, will you please, Nancy, and then you stay too. I want to get this straightened out. I've got enough trouble with squabbling teenagers at home. I don't need it here at the office."

When both Tom and I were seated in the office, and the door was closed, Tom said, "Is this a sales meeting? Are we going to add Nancy to the sales staff? I'll bet she could sell insurance to the dead with her personality."

"Come on, Tom, you know it's about that darned pipe of yours. Why do you like to annoy Nancy with it? She's got our sales records in the best order ever, and I want her to be happy here."

Still smoking his pipe, Tom went behind Mr. Jones' desk and opened the window. He looked directly at me and said, "I've been working here for eight years, smoking my pipe for eight years, and selling lots of insurance for eight years."

He turned toward Mr. Jones and said, "Is a clerk more important to you than I am?"

Mr. Jones began to squirm in his chair, and I was about to say

I'd figure out some way to live with the problem. I knew Mr. Jones couldn't afford to lose Tom, and I wanted to keep my job.

"Wait a minute," Tom said, apparently wanting to end Mr. Jones' discomfort. "That sounded too much like a threat. I like it here, I like you, boss, and I'm not going to run off and sell insurance for someone else. There's a simple solution to this problem: all these pure air nuts are creating everywhere. It's ventilation. All we've got to do is create ventilation, and everyone will be happy."

Mr. Jones' phone rang just then, and he waved us out of the office after he began talking to whoever was on the other end.

"Must be a big customer to be even more important than our pressing problem," Tom said as he opened the office door and bowed me through first.

Since that confrontation two weeks ago, Tom has had some fun with his proposed solution to the problem of his smoke and my complaining.

The next day he had the smallest fan I've ever seen on his desk. When he came into the office in the afternoon and lit his pipe, he turned on the tiny fan. It did blow some of the smoke up and away from me. I turned my back to him and pretended he wasn't there.

We ate in silence in the restaurant until Tom said, "You know, there is a reason I like to smoke and relax in the office. I had to quit smoking when I called on customers. So when I get back to the office, I'm ready for a good smoke."

I thought of my husband and how he enjoyed smoking after a meal or while watching television. For that matter, he seemed to enjoy it any time.

"Why do you have to smoke at all," I said. "It's not good for you. My husband died from it."

Tom leaned back in his chair and looked at me as though he was about to explain something to a child.

"Come now, did your husband really die from smoking?" "He died from lung cancer," I said, "but his smoking was the cause."

Tom leaned forward in his chair and said, "Well, in any event,

I'm sorry. But I doubt that smoking was the major cause of his death. I know smoking, especially cigarettes, has been linked to cancer. Still, people get cancer without smoking, and all people who smoke don't get cancer."

"Does anyone ever win an argument with you?" I said, wanting to change the subject. I enjoyed dining with someone and didn't want it to become more grieving for my husband. I couldn't seem to get over it, but it was out of my mind for a few minutes while arguing with Tom.

"I guess I am opinionated about all these health nuts and their ideas. It makes you wonder if it would be worth living if you followed all the don'ts."

We finished our meals, paid our bills, and walked back to the parking lot when Tom said, "How are you coping with living alone? It's beginning to get me down. Funny, I always thought being alone with my freedom was just what I wanted, and it was fine for the last few years, but now, I don't know."

We walked another half a block before I said, "Well, it wasn't any problem at first. I was so grieved over my husband's death that having people around was uncomfortable. But now I'm beginning to feel, oh, I don't know, restless, I guess. I can't go on grieving forever. After all, I'm only 32 years old. There must be something more to life."

Why had I told him that? It wasn't true. He wasn't exactly a stranger, but why should I be telling him how I felt and lying about it at that?

"That's kind of the way it is with me," Tom said as his shoulder brushed mine and grabbed my arm to keep me from staggering off the sidewalk. "Sorry, I didn't mean to knock you down."

As we continued, he was filling his pipe, and I wondered what he was restless about but decided not to ask.

"It isn't that I had anything to grieve about, like a real loss or anything. But, I'm tired of nightclubs, picking up stray women, and all that stuff that seemed so great before."

"How old are you," I asked. When he told me he was 33, I said, "It's easy to see what's happening to you. You're just ready to settle down."

He laughed and agreed that maybe he was. We talked and smiled, and I enjoyed it more than anything I'd experienced since my husband died.

"That little fan I had on my desk was just a gag. We're going to put in an entire ventilation system that will take the smoke right to the ceiling and out of the room," he said as we reached the parking lot.

Our parting seemed a little awkward. I felt he wanted to kiss me, but I was glad he didn't. I wouldn't have known how to react.

I slept the best I had in a long time that night, but in the morning, when I was getting ready to go to work, I still had that feeling of dislike as I looked at myself in the minor.

I didn't see Tom that day and was annoyed with myself because it seemed to matter.

But the next day, he came into the office in the afternoon and stayed there until we closed. He only lit up his pipe once, and that silly little fan of his carried the smoke away from me.

Once when he was walking past my desk, near closing time, he dropped a piece of folded note paper into my in-coming basket. I felt like a schoolgirl as I looked around to see if anyone had noticed and then unfolded it.

"Are you hungry again tonight?" The note said. "If you are, how about joining me for dinner?" He signed it, "Practically Smokeless."

After thinking it over for nearly an hour, I wrote him a note agreeing to go to dinner with him and dropped it on his desk while he was talking to Mr. Jones.

After closing the office, he directed me to his car in the parking lot. He said this was going to be his treat all the way if it was alright with me.

Again I agreed, and he drove us to a fancy restaurant on the outskirts of town. *The Flamingo* featured bamboo and tropical scenes in dimly lit and quiet alcoves, perfect for private dining areas for each customer or group.

"This is where I bring women when I want to impress them,

and besides, I only live a few blocks from here. I'd like you to see my home."

I laughed nervously and said, "I will get something to eat first, won't I?'

He guaranteed it and began discussing the menu. After a while, he recommended the roast beef and a particular kind of wine I'd never heard of. I asked him to order for both of us.

An elderly male waiter, with a folded napkin hanging from his left arm, came to the table with two martinis after Tom pushed a button on the wall. He asked Tom how his roses were doing and took our order.

As he was about to leave, he turned to me, smiled, and said, "I hope you enjoy your dinner."

"He seems to be a friend of yours. I suppose you dine here often and have impressed him with your bevy of females. What's this about your roses?"

Tom said I'd have to wait and see. Before I was entirely through with my drink, another one appeared.

"It takes a while to prepare food the way they do here, so Jason, the waiter, always brings me two drinks while I'm waiting. If you don't want to drink it, you don't have to, of course." Tom said as he looked at me over the rim of his glass.

The stuffed chair I was sitting in seemed to be massaging my body as I stretched out my legs, sighed, and said, "I don't mind at all. It's so peaceful here. No telephones ringing, no smoke blowing in my face. I feel like taking off my shoes."

"Do it," Tom said. "That's the rule here, or at least it's my rule. Comfort and privacy. I slipped off my shoes when we first came in."

I didn't believe him, but he stuck a shoeless foot beside the table for me to see, and we both laughed over that.

Eventually, the meal came, and, as predicted, it was wonderful. The meat was tender and delicious, and the gravy was something that made you want the recipe. I'm sure the desserts offered were equally good, but I didn't find out that night because I was too stuffed to eat another bite.

"Don't forget your shoes," Tom said as we prepared to leave. "I almost did forget mine one night."

It was almost dark when we left, and as I realized Tom was driving to his home, I didn't even think of protesting. But I was shocked when I saw the house through the tangle of undergrowth in the front yard. Farm fields were on both sides, and it looked like something out of a horror movie as we drove up the gravel driveway and parked near the front door.

The house had once been painted white with green trim, but now the little paint left was peeling and faded.

"Doesn't look like much, does it," Tom said as he came to my side of the car and opened the door.

"It looks abandoned and like a sanctuary for ghosts," I said, not trying to conceal my disappointment. I don't know what I expected, but it wasn't this.

"Follow me to the back, and maybe you'll see a little of what I saw when I bought it two years ago," Tom said.

As we neared the back of the house, I could see that much work had been done in the yard. Mowed grass formed a soft carpet, and blocks of roses were scattered throughout the yard. A link fence surrounded everything, which was the exact opposite of the untended mess in front.

Tom led me to the middle of the yard, and there, a swing wide enough for two, swaying gently in the breeze under a roofed patio. We sat down, and as I looked at the back of the house, I could see the fresh paint glowing in the light of a moon that had started to climb behind us.

We must have talked there for an hour. Tom turned on a soft yellow light under the roof, and I could see some of the roses, especially the white ones. The blooms were large and perfect if the one Tom picked for me was any indication.

"The roses were here when I bought the place. I didn't notice them until I started cutting away the underbrush. And then I got hooked. I spent nearly the first summer here getting the backyard straightened out. It was something new for me. Since leaving home to go to college years ago, I hadn't cut the grass, and I never dreamed of becoming a gardening nut."

I was in for another surprise when Tom opened the back door and led me into a perfect modern kitchen. It was huge, with a gleaming white sink and spotless pots and pans hung above an electric stove that looked as though it had just come from the display window of a store.

'As you can see, I'm working from the back to the front. I don't have much more to show you. This is almost as far as I've gone," he said as he pulled out a cushioned kitchen chair and invited me to sit at the table that looked out into the backyard.

After praising the kitchen, I began talking about myself at his prompting. Telling him about my husband, who was a welder, how we were married shortly after high school and had kept putting off having children until we had enough money.

"You know," he said, "I'm something of a psychologist. It helps sell insurance if you can see where your customer is coming from. Anyway, I think you feel guilty about your husband's death. Maybe you think you could have prevented it if you had forced him to stop smoking. That's why you're so dead set against smoking now. Have you always been that way?"

Now the room was quiet. I didn't know what to say, and what he had said was ringing in my ears. Did I feel guilty about my husband's death?

I heard his chair scrape the floor as he moved away from the table. "I'll make us some coffee," he said.

I still wondered whether I felt responsible for my husband's death when he brought the coffee and said, "Do you want to stay for breakfast?"

It wasn't until I put the hot coffee to my lips that I realized what he had asked me. Did I want to stay for breakfast? Getting up and making breakfast for someone besides myself would be nice.

"We'd have to get up early," I said, "because I'd have to pick up my car and go home to change clothes before I went to work.

We agreed that wouldn't be a problem as he had an alarm clock. He said, "OK, you can sleep in the bedroom, and I'll sleep in my sleeping bag here in the kitchen."

"Have you ever had to do that before?" I asked and laughed at the look on his face when he admitted he hadn't.

Looking back, I don't know why I suddenly was so willing to sleep with him. It wasn't out of passion, although it certainly is now. I don't know; maybe I'd just decided to move on, and this was one way of doing it.

He turned off the kitchen lights, took my hand, and led me into the bedroom. "Nothing in here yet but the moonlight," he said. "I haven't gotten around to doing anything about the wiring in here."

But the moonlight was just right. It was dark enough to hide my embarrassment at undressing with a man other than my husband. Yet, there was enough light that I could see the outline of his body as he came toward me and took me into his arms.

I'll never forget the feeling of his hard body against my nakedness. The lack of passion ended as we rolled onto the bed and lost ourselves in each other. Later, as I lay exhausted, the moonlight gave the room a gold-like glow. I went to sleep feeling as though I was floating on a gently bobbing golden boat.

The sun was beginning to creep into the room when I awakened. I slipped out of bed and took the alarm clock to the window, where I saw that it was five a.m., an hour before Tom had set the alarm. I turned off the alarm, took my clothes to the kitchen, and dressed as I watched the shadows gradually disappear from the backyard.

Later, as I was preparing breakfast, I realized I was humming to myself. As the bacon sizzled, I wondered whether Tom had set this whole thing up just so he could get me in bed.

Was I going to get hurt? What kind of woman would go to bed with him like I did? Was he sincere about wanting to settle down?

The questions tumbled over each other as I found the bathroom and turned on the light. Soon I would wake Tom and offer him breakfast. Why did I feel so good when I had doubts about his intentions?

I didn't get definite answers after I washed my face and looked in the mirror. But I did get another surprise. I was smiling at myself. My face looked pretty again. And my eyes sparkled. What had happened to that grim face I'd been wakening up to since my husband's death?

Maybe Tom was right. Maybe I felt guilty about my husband's death because I didn't stop him from smoking. But I couldn't have forced him to stop smoking any more than I could have forced him to stop breathing the fumes from his welding job. It wasn't my fault he had died.

Later I woke Tom with a feeling that this was the first day of the rest of my life and that it would be good.

MY SISTER'S WEDDING

By **BOB LITER**, edited by Martie Liter Ogborn

"I'm surprised at you, Martie," Ginny said as she sat across from me in Monica's Restaurant. I picked at my lettuce salad and thought of how I'd like to binge on mashed potatoes and gravy, lots of fattening gravy.

"What?" I said as my mind returned to reality.

"You're jealous of your sister. Don't deny it."

I put my fork down. I'd given my husband two fine children. Why did I have to diet and ride that darned exercise bike? He was more interested in my sister's wedding than in me anyway.

I said, "Let's have dessert. Something good! Of course, it'll be fattening. If it's good, it's fattening."

Ginny, Virginia Barker, my best friend, stuffed the last bite of pasta in her mouth, chewed it thoroughly, and said, "You're ignoring the subject."

"And the subject is?"

"You're jealous of your sister."

"Why should I be jealous of Jeannie? I'm happy for her. She's getting married in a church with our parents and relatives there. I got married at city hall with no flowers and a license in my hand. Why should I be jealous?"

"As I remember, you were a sunbeam that day you and Jerry married. You didn't say anything about wanting a fancy wedding then. Jerry was so handsome, so eager to marry you.

You were the happiest girl in the world."

She was right. We were married while he was studying computer science at Illinois Central College. I was a waitress. I didn't care about marrying in a church with all the trimmings. I just wanted to be married.

Three days after having lunch with Ginny, I was with my sister, Jeannie, at The Wedding Boutique in Westgate Shopping Center. The wedding consultant, Agnes, who had never been married, tried for the third time in a week to convince Jeannie that a Princess dress was just right for her.

Jeannie, her eyes shining and cheeks flushed, said, "What do you think, Martie? You try it on so I can really see it."

"That's a good idea," Agnes said. "Jeannie can get a better picture that way."

Better picture? Jeannie had looked at herself in the dress often enough to draw a picture!

My protests were ignored, and finally, to get the business over with, I went into the changing room and slipped into the dress. I had felt happy for Jeannie, but now, jealousy returned as I stepped before them and turned like a model.

I felt like crying. I was so ashamed because of my feelings.

"My God, Martie! You look gorgeous, just gorgeous," Jeannie said.

I suppose I blushed. My little sister said I looked gorgeous. She's the one who looked gorgeous, always had. And ever since her wedding was announced, she'd taken on a special glow.

Agnes gazed up and down at the dress and circled around me.

"It's nearly perfect," she said. "Maybe I'll let it out just a bit at the waist."

"Don't be silly," I said. "Jeannie still has her girlish figure. You won't need to let it out."

"Oh, of course not," Agnes said. "I'm such a nut. When someone puts on a dress, I automatically start thinking of what alterations will be needed. Sorry."

She circled me again and looked at Jeannie.

"It's just perfect. Thanks for modeling it for me."

I said, "Hey, no problem. Do you still want me to wear my evening gown? The one I wore to Jerry's promotion dinner."

"Sure. Why spend money on another one? You'll look beautiful."

I felt left out as Jeannie and Agnes whispered while glancing my way. I heard Agnes say, "Don't worry about it. I'll send all the bills to him."

Poor Harold, Jeannie's fiancé. How was he going to pay for everything? Well, it was his and Jeannie's wedding. If they wanted to go into debt, what business was it of mine?

The day of the wedding finally arrived. They insisted Jerry and I get there early.

"Don't worry about the boys. We'll get them there on time," my mother, Lillian, said. She and my dad, Bob, were always there when we needed extra help with the kids.

Mom looked great. Still, slim, silver-white hair cut short, and dad was as dapper as ever. I hoped I looked that good when I reached their ages.

Jerry was in a tux, and our sons, looking much older, were in their miniature matching tuxedos. It made me proud and sad at the same time. They were growing up so fast. Scott, the youngest, was to be the ring bearer. Rob, our oldest son, named after my dad, coached Scott on how to do it.

I was ushered into a meeting room at the church, and the door was closed. Ginny and Jeannie were there. Jeannie, already in her wedding gown, walked back and forth.

Ginny handed me a garment bag from The Wedding Boutique and said, "Martie, you've got to put this on one more time, so I can get a picture of the two of you."

"What? You don't even have a camera," I said.

Jeannie, still pacing, said, "We've got to tell her. We can't wait any longer." She stopped before Ginny and said, "You tell her!"

"No, this is family. You tell her!"

I stamped my foot. "Tell me what?"

Jeannie took a deep breath and said, "All right, if it will get you to change, I'll tell you."

She unzipped the garment bag, produced a duplicate of her wedding dress, and told me to put it on.

"Jerry is paying for the weddings," she said.

"Jerry is WHAT!" I said.

"She said weddingS, Martie," Ginny Barker said, with a smile on her face as big as Texas. "So let's get with it, change into YOUR wedding dress, go out there, and smile. You and Jerry repeat your wedding vows while Jeannie and Harold say their wedding vows for the first time."

Our dad, Bob Liter, was waiting to walk Jeannie and me down the aisle to our "happily-ever-afters."

THE RESCUE
By **BOB LITER**

Alice Turnbull placed her elbows on the library table, leaned forward, and covered her eyes with her hands.

A book, *The Life and Times of Millicent Avery*, lay before her. She had opened the book to page 75, where she'd stopped the day before.

Now she had read to page 120 about a young woman's struggle to survive in a sod hut on the Nebraska prairie in 1888. The woman had been left alone when her husband died of pneumonia. She survived winter storm after winter storm and eventually married again, raised four children, and became a force in the developing community.

Alice knew about being alone. She sighed and opened the book again, gazed at page 121 without reading, closed it, got up, returned it to its shelf, and wandered outside. She could check the book out, but if she did, she'd have no reason to leave her apartment now that she was on summer vacation.

She loved teaching high school history, but summer vacations were always disappointing after the first week. As usual, she spent her time reading American history in the library. She admired women like Millicent Avery and enjoyed reading about them. Still, she knew it was a substitute for having a life of her own.

What about her sister, her sister's husband, and their two

children? She would visit them next month. In the meantime, she and her friend would go to Monica's Restaurant, as they did most every week, overeat and go to a movie.

She stood in front of the library, stretched, looked at the few fluffy clouds drifting by, and felt a pleasant breeze kiss her cheek. Arnold Street traffic pounded past. A child flashed from behind her toward the curb as a small ball bounced into the street. She took three quick steps and jerked the girl back from the curb.

"What's the matter with you, child? You could have been killed," Alice said in her most severe classroom voice.

Tears welled in the child's eyes. She howled and tried to pull her hand away from Alice. A tall man, arms filled with books, kneeled in front of the child, placed the books on the sidewalk, and held her to his chest.

"What's the matter, Pumpkin? Don't cry. You shouldn't run ahead. I've told you about that."

"I dropped my ball. It's gone. This lady scolded me."

The man picked up the child, stroked her light brown hair with his long, slender fingers, and focused his blue-gray eyes on Alice.

"I stopped her from running into the street. She could have been killed. Why do you let her run loose with all this traffic around?"

"Did you ever try to control a six-year-old child whose mother lets her have her own way? Besides, I had my arms full of books."

Alice bristled. She had controlled a roomful of such children. She bit her lip to keep from saying so. The man set the child on the ground, stretched to six feet or more, and said, "Now, you stay right here until I pick up the books. Then we'll go get something to eat. You should thank the lady. You might have been killed."

Alice admired the man's neatly trimmed graying hair, lean face, and square jaw.

"Can I have a hamburger, gramps? I'm hungry."

So, he was her grandfather. He looked to be about forty, about Alice's age.

The man sighed and said, "I've forgotten whatever I knew about taking care of a child. Is there a good place around here we could eat?"

Alice hesitated. She planned to walk to the Quick Cafe and order her usual salad. Should she recommend the place? Why not? Walking with the man and his granddaughter to the cafe wouldn't hurt. She pointed up the block.

"Thank you," he said. He and the girl were beside her as Alice walked toward the cafe.

"My name's Henry Dawson, Hank, and this is my granddaughter, Catherine. We call her Kitty."

He stopped and extended his hand. Alice extended hers. They shook formally.

"I'm Alice Turnbull. Glad to meet you both," Alice said.

Kitty held out her hand. Alice leaned over and took it.

She initially felt uncomfortable when they sat together at the only empty booth in the cafe. Kitty ordered a hamburger, french fries, and root beer. Hank insisted she have milk.

"You come to the library often?" Hank said.

"Yes, most days. I'm a school teacher. On summer vacation."

"I'm on vacation myself. Promised my daughter-in-law I'd take Kitty to the library. It could have been a disaster if you hadn't ... "

"What do you do?" Alice asked.

"I'm an instructor at the junior college. Teach woodworking, mostly. My wife died two years ago."

The food came. Kitty chattered between bites. Hank gave her one of the library books. She opened it and was quiet for a minute.

"We must return to the library next week to bring the books back. Will you be there?" Hank asked.

Alice looked at Hank and back at the child.

"Yes, I'll probably be there," she said.

"Could we have lunch again?" Kitty said.

"Well, I ... "

"A great idea, Kit," Hank said.

Alice dabbed at her salad. Kitty swallowed the last of her milk and said, "Come on, gramps. I want to go home and read my books."

Kitty scooted out of the booth, and Hank followed. He stood in front of Alice with his arms full of books.

Alice said, "Yes, we could meet again next Friday. I'd like that."

"So would I," Hank said. "Maybe then I could get your phone number?"

PRESSURE POINT
By **BOB LITER**

Nurse Cindy Jones sighed as she sat on the edge of a Methodist hospital bed, applying pressure to the inside of the man's groin. He was back from an angiogram.

For twenty minutes, she could stop hurrying from one task to another while preventing the small wound from bleeding.

The patient was quiet, like Billy. Now, what made her think of that? It was twelve years since Billy Canfield, her fiancé, was killed in Kuwait. Now, at night, before she slept, she'd remember the feel of his lips, the feel of his touch. But sometimes, she couldn't bring up an image of his face.

The following day, she would often study the photographs of him she kept in the living room.

Returning to the present, she asked the patient, "You doing all right?"

He turned his lined face toward her and said, "Yeah, sure. How much longer do I have to stay here?"

"We've got to ensure you don't bleed where the catheter was inserted. That's why I'm applying pressure, so the opening can seal itself. It'll only take another ten minutes or so. But you'll stay for at least three hours. Keep your leg still and straight, please."

The man, Mr. Andrews, sighed and said, "I'm too weak from lack of food to move anything."

Fifteen more minutes and her shift would be over. Cindy looked at the bed, a bed like all the others in the hospital. White sheets, sideboards, and levers to elevate and lower the patient. When she stopped applying pressure, the bandage she would put on the wound was on a portable table, safe in its sterile package.

She occasionally heard activity in the hallway behind her, but no sound in the room except her breathing and the man's breathing. How often had she sat on the edge of a hospital bed and leaned her hand on a patient's inner thigh? Her life had become limited to going to work, returning to her quiet apartment, and going to work.

Sure, she had friends at the hospital, primarily nurses, mostly married. But they had stopped inviting her to join them for a girls' night out. She'd refused too many times.

"Hi Danny," the patient said as he looked over her shoulder.

A deep, strong voice behind her said, "Jean called me. Asked me to take you home. How come I find out you're in the hospital from my sister?"

The patient moved. "No, no, Mr. Andrews. You must lie still; keep your leg flat until . . ."

He settled down and said, "I had a chance to get this done today when the doctor had an opening. They told me not to eat or drink anything. Now I'm starving. What time is it?"

"Nearly five," the younger man said. He had blue eyes and a strong chin, a younger version of the patient.

"I'm sure something to eat will be here soon," Cindy said. "Please lie still."

"My son, Danny," Mr. Andrews said.

The son nodded toward Cindy, leaned over, and patted his father's hand. The son straightened, his eyes focused on hers.

Her free hand went to her hair, pushing a bit off her forehead. She thought *I should have put on some makeup, a little eye shadow, or something.* At least she had washed her hair the night before. She had combed and arranged the unruly brown waves that morning but knew they were out of control by now.

Dirt smudges marked the son's white T-shirt. It was wet, as though he'd been sweating, and his muscular chest might as well have been naked, the way it revealed itself through the thin material.

He grabbed a cushioned chair from the corner and flipped it beside the bed. His eyes engaged hers again. It was like a caress.

"So tell me what's going on," he said to his father.

"Just an angiogram. Gonna get something done about my leg cramps. Can't even mow the yard without stopping to ease the pain."

"What's an angiogram?"

"Ask her?"

Cindy kept the pressure on Mr. Andrew's groin. She said, "An angiogram is a series of x-ray pictures to show the doctor where the circulation blockage is. That's what causes the pain. Dye is injected into the blood vessels through a catheter to enhance the pictures. You should ask the doctor."

"You all right, Pop?"

"Sure, I'm fine. Warm now. It was colder than hell in that place where they took me. All kinds of machines; kind of a scary place. They said they had to keep it cool for the machinery. What about the patients?"

"Didn't they put a warmed blanket over you?" Cindy said.

"Yeah, they did do that."

The son smiled at her with his close-cropped brown hair and expressive lips that curled over white, even teeth. His eyes twinkled like the patient's. What did he think she would do, swoon?

"You got a girl yet?" the patient asked his son.

"You're worse than mom used to be. You'll have your grandchild sooner or later. I just haven't had time to meet the right woman."

"You should take the time. You're not getting any younger, you know."

"Yes, mother," the young man said with love in his voice.

"I'm sure your food will be here soon," Cindy said. She released the pressure on her patient's groin. She opened the bandage package, applied the bandage to the wound, and taped it in place. She patted the patient's hand and continued, "I'll check on the food to make sure."

She glanced at the younger man, Danny. It must be what his father called him since he was a little boy. She couldn't think of him as anything but Dan. Why should she think of him at all?

"How's the construction business?" Mr. Andrews said.

"Still constructing," Dan said. "Building a retaining wall now at one of those fancy homes out in Peoria Heights."

She was on her way out of the room when she heard Dan say, "Since you're going to be here awhile, guess I'll find the cafeteria and get something to eat."

Cindy turned at the doorway and said, "The cafeteria's on the third floor. There's an elevator down the hall to the right."

"Thanks," Dan said. She was still seeing his smile when she reached the nurse's station.

Rose Blant, the head nurse on the floor, said, "Well, why the mysterious smile? Time for you to get off already?"

"Yeah, already," Cindy said. "I've been here since seven this morning, as you well know."

"Go on then," Rose said. "I'll see you Thursday."

Cindy got her purse from the locker and hurried to the elevator. She pushed the down button, but when the elevator arrived, she shook her head even though no one was there. She pushed the up button. When another elevator arrived, she entered it and pushed the third-floor button.

Alone in the elevator, she said aloud, "What am I doing? I've got food at home."

She'd go back down to the first floor and out to her old Chevy. She'd go home and eat another TV dinner.

The elevator stopped on the third floor. The door slid open. She didn't move. Her hand shot out and stopped the door before it closed. Outside, she hesitated, walked to the right, past the Image Department, and entered the long hallway to the cafeteria. Still, time to turn back. But why? She had a right to eat in the cafeteria if she wanted.

She took a tray and moved slowly down the cafeteria line. So much to choose from. All kinds of goodies. You'd think they wouldn't offer so much fattening food in a hospital where they're telling patients to stick to a proper diet. A salad, that's what she'd have. And maybe a piece of cake. No, no cake. Why not? She hadn't had a piece of cake for a week. And the chocolate cake looked so good.

She added a cup of coffee to her tray, nodded to the checkout girl, paid her, and stepped away. Only a few of the several tables were unoccupied. Dan sat alone near the picture window, looking at the street below.

He jumped up, covered the distance between them in a few strides, and said, "Here, let me take your tray. I hate eating alone."

He snatched it, turned, and walked back to his table. She followed, hesitated, and sat down.

"My name's Cindy," she said.

"I know."

Her body relaxed. She looked at this handsome man, this man who seemed interested in her, and smiled.

"Nice smile," Dan said.

"Thanks," Cindy said.

"I'm thinking of asking you out," he added.

After a few seconds of indecision, Cindy said, "If you ask me, I'm thinking of saying yes."

TUMBLEWEED AND GOOSEBERRY PIE

By **BOB LITER**, Edited by Martie Liter Ogborn

"What's ya doin', Mr. Dump?" Johnny Andrews asked. Billy Gombeski grinned.

"Minding my own business," Ezra Dumpfeld said. "You kids get upstairs where you belong."

Ezra shook his head and leaned against the workbench in his space off the furnace room of Central City's Warren Harding Elementary School. He poured freshly made coffee into a stained cup and avoided the chipped part of the rim as he sipped suspiciously. Tasted all right. Not like it did the other day when one of the kids put pepper in his coffee pot.

He turned to the pile of tumbleweeds he'd gathered that morning from the schoolyard before the kids arrived. He picked up one of the ball-shaped weeds after opening the door to the ancient iron coal-burning furnace. The weeds would probably burn hot, maybe stink up the place again. He should have left them outside and burned them there, but then he'd probably get chewed out because of the danger of starting a prairie fire.

He slapped his forehead and started crushing the weeds in a bucket. Why hadn't he thought of this before? He put them in his ancient food blender and turned them to powder.

Ezra chuckled as he thought of how he would trick Mrs.

Murdock and get even with all the smartass kids continually harassing him. And, it would serve Mrs. Murdock right to complain because he wasn't keeping her kitchen clean enough.

Just before lunch, he carried a broom into the kitchen. Mrs. Murdock sat at the cutting table, slicing carrots. Her bulk spilled over the edges of the stool. Ezra turned his back to her and pulled a plastic sandwich bag of tumbleweed powder from inside his bib overalls. He dumped the powder into a large aluminum pot filled with chicken and noodle soup. He stirred it with a wooden spoon until she said, "Take your dirty overalls and grimy hands out of my kitchen. You are always hanging around when I'm working. Spend more time here cleaning after I'm gone for the day."

"Thought you might give me a little something to eat."

"Not likely, you old goat. Now git."

After lunch, Ezra was disappointed when no one complained about the soup. Still, he had put something over on the whole school. He tasted the leftover soup later, and it tasted like always. He ground up more tumbleweed and smiled as he sneaked some in Mrs. Murdock's soup every day. Gradually she didn't seem to mind him being there. He felt guilty a week later when Mrs. Murdock made him a gooseberry pie. While eating a piece, Mr. Anders, the principal, came in before Ezra could jump up and pretend to be working.

"Ah, Mr. Dumpfeld," he said.

Here it comes, Ezra figured. He's gonna chew me out for being here instead of working.

"I've been meaning to tell you what a good job you've been doing lately," Mr. Anders said. Ezra choked and almost lost a mouthful of pie. Mr. Anders got himself a plate, cut a piece, and ate it when Mrs. Murdock returned from the restroom.

"I was just gonna run him outta here," Mrs. Murdock said.

"Oh, don't do that. Let him enjoy this delicious pie. Your food has been extra good lately, excellent in fact," Mr. Anders said.

Winter came as fast as usual on the prairie; snow buried the tumbleweeds and nearly everything else. Ezra hated shoveling snow. To his suspicious surprise, some of the boys helped him. In the meantime, he figured it was time he complimented Mrs. Murdock on her cooking. But she was harping at him again before he got around to it. And kids were calling him Mr. Dump again and trashing the schoolrooms. No more help shoveling snow, either.

At the first hint of spring, Ezra gathered a few tumbleweeds that had freed themselves from snowdrifts and blown into the schoolyard. He was about to burn them when he decided to make more powder and put it in the soup. It would be his secret again.

Two weeks later, the kids stopped making fun of him, and Mrs. Murdock let him hang around her kitchen. She even smiled sometimes and made him another gooseberry pie. They were all so nice he stopped putting tumbleweed powder in their soup. Soon the kids called him Mr. Dump, and Mrs. Murdock told him to stay out of her kitchen. He scratched his head as he crushed more tumbleweed and figured he'd get even by putting the powder in their soup.

THE WAITRESS

By **BOB LITER**, Edited by Martie Liter Ogborn

Monica Arnold slid off the counter stool, placed her feet carefully on the floor, and walked across Gina's Diner to the two women sitting in the window booth. She refilled their coffee cups and did the same at the next two booths.

"I see your special didn't show up today?" Vicki Brattle said when Monica returned to the counter. A toothy grin lit up Vicki's face as she wrapped thin arms around her chest. "Where do you suppose he is?"

Yes, Mr. Ackerman hadn't shown up. Strange. He had been coming in daily around noon for a month or so. He always sat at the corner booth and ordered the special. He ate without enthusiasm, nodded when Monica asked him if everything was okay, and left a two-dollar tip.

Waiting for Gina Springfield, the cook and diner owner, to dish up another order, Monica sat, wiggled her toes, and thought about Mr. Ackerman. A scraggly beard partially hid his face, his clothes were wrinkled and baggy, and his eyes were clouded with sadness.

Vicki called him her special customer. Special? Nothing special about him. Still, she was vaguely worried because he didn't show.

Gina came out of the kitchen and settled her ample bottom on a stool beside Monica. Monica started to get up.

"No, stay a minute. Did Mr. Ackerman say anything yesterday?"

Monica shook her head. "He never says anything."

Gina swallowed iced water and said, "I knew his wife slightly from high school. Her obituary was in the paper. They didn't have any children."

Monica turned. "Her death must be why he looks so sad and has let himself go. The poor man. Still, he should pull himself together. I hope he's all right."

"Your special customer probably found a new place to eat and a new waitress," Vicki said as she stood behind them.

"Don't listen to her, Monica. She's just jealous because she doesn't have a special customer," Gina said.

Monica carried a couple of hamburgers to the women at table five, returned for more coffee, refilled more cups, and resumed sitting at the counter.

"Jealous," Vicki said. "Who's jealous of an old man who wears baggy clothes, always needs a shave, and looks like Mr. Sad Sack himself?"

"Old? He's not much over forty. He just let himself go after his wife died," Gina said.

Vicki drained her glass of Pepsi and said, "How do you know his wife died? Don't believe everything these guys say."

Gina said, "His wife did die. I saw the obituary in the paper."

"Well, speak of the devil. Here he is," Vicki said.

Monica straightened her uniform and grabbed her order pad from the counter. She stood in front of Mr. Ackerman at the corner booth and said, "What'll it be today?"

"The special."

"Its sauerkraut and wieners," Monica said.

"Okay. And coffee."

Monica hesitated, feeling she should say something that might cheer him up. But what? He looked at her as if to say, "You still here?"

She waited on other customers, brought his food, and returned to the counter. He finished the meal in silence, except when he said, "Thanks," after she refilled his coffee cup. He left the usual two-dollar tip.

A couple of hours later, her shift was over, she'd made thirty dollars in tips, and her feet hurt. This was the night she would get out of her apartment for once and go to a movie. Maybe tomorrow, she decided. She walked the two blocks to Restful Arms, took the elevator to the third floor, trudged down the hall to Unit 312, unlocked the door, and entered. She flopped into the worn easy chair in front of the portable TV and sighed. She kicked off her shoes, wiggled her toes, and closed her eyes.

You never do anything except go to work, come home, wash your uniforms, stare at the TV, and sleep.

She was talking to herself again. She hadn't always been alone. She turned and looked at the shelf on the far wall. The best photo of her mother, when she was young and smiling, looked back at her.

Her mother. How long had she been gone now? Three years? Yes, three years. Monica had cared for her mother for twenty years. She felt a burden lift from her when a third heart attack ended her mother's life. She was ashamed of the feeling, but she couldn't help it.

She had been tied down for so long. No love life, no adventure. How could she have any of that when she was sentenced to care for her sick mother? Her mother, who had raised her with loving care, never complained until the last couple of years.

Monica earned a meager living at Gina's Diner. She'd been a waitress all those years, but why was she still there? Was she afraid of change?

It was midnight when she awoke, still in the chair, hungry and stiff. She stumbled to bed.

At work the next day, a man who looked familiar came in and sat at the corner booth, Mr. Ackerman's booth. Monica carried a menu and a glass of water, sat the water down in front of the man, and said, "Hello, the special today is homemade meatloaf and mashed potatoes."

The man looked up at her, smiled, and said, "I'll have that."

Monica's hand went to her open mouth. It was Mr. Ackerman. His eyes were as sad as ever, but he had shaved, gotten a haircut, and wore wrinkle-free clothes.

"Mr. Ackerman?"

"Yes. It's me. I'm moving on. My wife always took care of me and kept after me to shave and get a haircut. Without her, I let go. It's hard, you know."

"I can imagine," Monica said.

His hairline left him with a lot of forehead, and his chin sort of caved in. Parallel creases topped his dark eyebrows. He raised them now as he said, "I been thinking of asking you for a date. Don't suppose a pretty woman like you would go out with the likes of me?"

Monica dropped her order pad, stooped, picked it up, and said, "I'll be right back with your lunch."

Her hands shook as she carried the order to his booth. She sat the food down and said, "I don't know. I don't go out much. Where'd we go?"

He smiled. She liked his smile. A person hardly noticed the dark tooth near the center of his mouth. And his eyes sort of lit up for an instant.

"We could go to a movie. Get to know each other. Wouldn't have to stay out late."

The date was uncomfortable at first. The movie was nothing special, something about a South American revolution. They had walked from the diner when Monica got off work. He appeared as uncomfortable as she felt. He did say, "Hope you like the movie," and she said, "Oh, I'm sure I will."

Outside, after it was over, they stood in front of the Crescent Theatre and looked at the posters of coming attractions.

"I was wondering," Mr. Ackerman said, "if you would like to work for me, be my housekeeper?"

Monica put her hands behind her back and walked toward her apartment. Mr. Ackerman followed.

"It'll feel good when I get home and take off my shoes," she said.

"If you kept house for me, your feet wouldn't take such a beating."

Mr. Ackerman took her hand when they crossed Elmhurst Street. She liked the feeling of that. Keep house for him? What would that entail? What would he pay?"

She asked the questions, surprised she could be so forthright.

"Well, I could pay as much as you get at the diner. You could come in the morning, do what little cleaning had to be done, run errands like getting my clothes from the cleaner, grocery shopping, stuff like that. Oh, and fix the meals."

"Where would you be? What kind of work do you do?"

Mr. Ackerman continued to hold her hand after they crossed the street.

"I operate a business on the Internet. Buy stuff, sell stuff. Used to have a regular store, but when my wife got sick, I had to operate at home."

It turned out Mr. Ackerman lived only two blocks from Monica. She said she would consider the job offer and let him know the next day. But she didn't wait.

"I'll do it. I've wanted to do something different ever since my mother died. I'll have to give a two-week notice."

Mr. Ackerman stopped walking, faced her, still holding her hand, and said, "This is great. Almost like a proposal. I should have a ring to put on your finger."

She hoped he didn't notice the blush she knew appeared on her face. At home, after he had kissed her on the cheek and said, "Goodnight," Monica wondered if she had done the right thing.

Four months later, when he proposed marriage, and she accepted, she still wondered if she was doing the right thing.

"Thanks for bringing my slippers," Mr. Ackerman said the day after the bare-bones wedding. Have you been to the cleaners yet? And I've got some dirty clothes in the hamper."

A few weeks later, Monica visited the diner. Vicki placed her hands on her hips and said, "Well, Mrs. Ackerman, is that guy taking care of you?"

"Not exactly," Monica said. "But it's easier on my feet."

NOW I'M TALKING
By BOB LITER

"You look better, Millie, but I'm still worried about you."

I shushed Joyce and gazed straight ahead, intent on hearing Jason Pollard read the opening chapter of his latest romance. We were among about twenty women in the conference room of Central City's Edgerton Book Store.

Pollard, a man of medium height with a flattened nose, was not at all like the hero of his novels, Jake Evert, who swept women off their feet and righted the wrongs of the world.

My disappointment in his appearance was similar to my empty feeling when I reached the end of each of his novels. Why couldn't the stories go on forever?

Now he was promoting his latest novel, and I would get in line and buy a copy as soon as his presentation was over. The reading and question-and-answer period ended too soon. I turned and faced Joyce.

"What were you saying?"

"I said you look better. When I left on vacation, you still looked like a zombie. What have you done to your hair?"

"How was California?" I asked.

"California was fine. What have you done to your hair?"

I combed my fingers through it and said, "Had it cut and colored. I've got a job, too. I work here during the day stacking books on the shelves when they come in."

Joyce parked on a folding chair beside mine.

"You're all right then, now that the divorce is final?"

I sat down, sighed, and said, "Yes, I think so."

Joyce leaned closer and said, "You think so?"

"Don't worry. I love this job. And I have a little money from the settlement. Enough to go on a trip if I want. I'm going to night school to learn to be a librarian."

"I'm sorry, Millie. You're putting on a brave front, but I don't believe you. You look better, but you still have that sad, far-away look in your eyes. Like you're lost."

I said. "Life goes on. I've got to get a copy of Mr. Pollard's new book."

The line, which had stretched from the table in front of the room to the back, had dwindled. Still, I sat there. What would I say to him? Maybe I'd just read the book. I didn't need his signature.

When the last buyer left, Mr. Pollard stood, stretched, and gathered up the few remaining copies of his book. He strolled up the aisle, looking lonely...

As he passed, Joyce stood and said, "We'd like to buy a book, or rather she would." She nodded toward me.

Mr. Pollard's warm smile was directed right at me.

"I've got to get going," Joyce said. "Call you tomorrow about tomorrow."

Mr. Pollard put the books on the chair Joyce had vacated, turned to me, smiled again, and said, "I hope you enjoy the book. How shall I sign it?"

I hesitated and finally said, "My name's Millie, Millie Strand. I've read all of your books. I just love 'em."

"Really. How nice. That's the best thing an author can hear."

He pulled up a chair, sat down, took the top book from the pile, and opened it.

"I'll sign it, To Millie, one of my favorite readers," he said.

I thanked him.

"I suppose you're disappointed I don't look like Jake."

"Jake?" I asked as if I didn't know.

"The guy who gets all the women. The hero of my books."

"Oh, of course. How stupid. Yes, you don't look like I imagine Jake does, but then . . ." I laughed weakly. "But then who does?"

He handed me the signed book, thanked me again, and picked up the others. He took a few steps away, paused, and turned.

"I don't suppose," he hesitated, "I don't suppose you'd have dinner with me. This is a lonely business, driving from city to city selling my books. I've been on the road two weeks now, and I'm really sick of eating alone."

I opened the book he'd handed me, looked at the signature, and finally said, 'Well, I don't know."

"Of course, if you're busy."

"It's not that. I'm not busy. Where would you want to eat?"

He smiled. "Hey, that'd be great. Any place you want."

"I don't go out much. My ex-husband and I used to eat at Harold's. It's not far from here. We could walk."

Harold's is one of those places with thick carpets, dim lighting, and tables far enough apart that you aren't bumping into your neighbor every time you move. The food is usually good.

After we were seated, I recovered from having nothing to say by asking, "How do you think of all the exciting stuff you put in your novels."

"A familiar question," he said. "It's a developed way of thinking. Newspapers, overheard conversations, our sitting here waiting for dinner, anything could be the start of a fictional idea."

"You had a scene in *Love Around the Corner* where the heroine ate dinner with a stranger."

"If you say so." He smiled. "I guess I did. The plots just sort of fade away from one story to another. Sometimes I have to check back to make sure I'm not telling the same story again."

Our food came. He stopped talking and cut his steak into little squares. He'd fork one, open his mouth, caress it with his lips and chew slowly.

"I haven't had time to eat all day," he said between bites.

I nibbled at my shrimp salad as he paused and said, "I'm

staying at the Carleton Hotel just around the corner. Would you like to come up and see my etchings?"

I smiled and continued to pick at the salad.

"I hope you're not offended," he said. "I was only kidding."

"Yeah, sure."

"Well, maybe not entirely, but I would like to see you again."

At lunch the next day, Joyce put her coffee cup down, leaned toward me, and said, "Did anything happen after I left?"

I smiled.

She said, "C'mon, what happened? You look younger, somehow."

"He said he would be coming back this way when he completed his tour. I wonder if he will. I gave him my phone number."

Joyce took my hand in hers, her big brown eyes wide with worry, and said, "Geez! Millie, if this guy never calls, I suppose it'll break your heart."

I smiled again.

"Why are you smiling?"

"Suppose he never calls. He made a pass at me. Maybe there'll be other passes by other guys now that I've come out of my shell. As a matter of fact, I've got my eye on the bookstore manager. He's not married and comes around daily and talks to me."

A grin spread across Joyce's face, and she said, "Now you're talking."

I thought about it and decided she was right. Now I was talking about getting on with my life.

IMPRESSING MARY LOW
By **BOB LITER**

I was nine years old when I struggled into my big brother Jay's skeleton costume. The black costume's white lines suggested bare, skinny bones. The face included a diabolical grin. Jay's frayed and dirt-smeared canvas tennies added what I thought was a scary touch.

I sneaked out of the house and crouched behind a bush near the front sidewalk. Buster, a little brown and white dog that got more attention from Mary Lou Fortino than I did, trotted by. I jumped out and growled. The trot became a mad dash preceded by a yelp.

Later, as I had hoped, Mary Lou came skipping down the sidewalk on her way to Jeannie Welk's home, where they played house and other girly stuff. Sunlight glanced off her shining, dark hair reflected from her brown eyes as she skipped along. I jumped in front of her and made what I imagined were skeleton noises. The oversized shoes became entangled, and I ended up sprawled on the sidewalk. She stepped around me, still skipping. The laughter faded as she continued down the walk without turning back.

Several days later, I was kicking a tattered soccer ball. She caught it when it skidded toward her. She gazed directly into my eyes as a beautiful smile spread across her face. She turned her head slowly from side to side and tossed the ball toward me. I stumbled and failed to catch it.

One of my attempts to impress her during high school involved a spotlight and a blown fuse. Mrs. Foster, the English and drama teacher, talked me into being a part of her variety show. I rehearsed it several times with the spotlight operator, Harry Will. He was supposed to direct the spot around the stage until it landed in my outstretched hand when I would stuff it in my pocket. The curtains rolled back, and Mrs. Foster shoved me on stage. I was numb with fright, but after a second or two of silence, I managed to call, "Here Spot."

Nothing happened. I called again, louder this time. Still nothing. People in the audience snickered and then laughed out loud. I mumbled, "I guess Spot's not here," and ran off the stage.

I got a big laugh from the audience of my classmates and their parents. I imagined I heard Mary Lou's voice among them. It did no good to explain what was supposed to happen and that a burned-out fuse put the spotlight out of business.

"Here Spot" was a typical comment for months afterward whenever most students came near me. But not Mary Lou; when we passed in the halls, she smiled and shook her head.

The basketball coach, Mr. Brand, said I could be a strong player the next semester because I was six feet tall by then. I didn't believe him, but Mary Lou was often seen with Brad Thomas, the team's star. So I went out for basketball. After a few days of stumbling around, I was sent in as the center during a scrimmage. Brad was the point guard; his job was to feed the ball to the other players when he wasn't making three-point shots.

He dribbled, passed, and moved so fast it was hard for me to keep track of him and at the same time move around near the basket like the coach said. I was backing against a defender near the basket when Brad whipped a pass in my direction. The ball bounced off my head. The practice stopped, and laughter erupted among the players and students scattered in the bleachers. I thought I heard Mary Lou's laughter, but I didn't have the nerve to look. Coach Brand led me off the court, insisted I sit, and practice resumed.

From then on, I shunned after-school activities. I even dropped out of the Science Club. I spent a lot of time in my room learning things from books and the computer and writing stuff. One of my letters was published by the local newspaper. It was about geopolitics and how it had meaning for everyone, even the citizens of our town. I wrote other letters. Soon most of them were published, and by my senior year in high school, I was a regular contributor. One letter about global warming was published by the Chicago Times.

My dad, a truck driver, and my Mom said they were proud of me. Still, the few kids at school who noticed seemed to think it was some nerdish thing that didn't compare with the ability to catch a ball of one kind or another.

Soon after World War II broke out, I joined the Navy. Nearly everybody was either drafted or joined up. I managed to get my hands on various science books. I studied hard even when I was seasick, which was most of the time. A month after being discharged, I entered the state university and wrote scientific articles for the college paper. Some of them were reprinted by other papers. I hoped Mary Lou was somehow aware of this, but I doubted it. Last I heard, she was dating various guys and studying journalism at Columbia in Missouri.

It was agony thinking about it. I supposed she was still wearing those tight, fuzzy sweaters that outlined her breasts. I had visions of her slender legs extending above bobby sox that had the privilege of caressing her ankles.

Eventually, I got so involved in my studies I didn't think about her for hours. By the time I earned a BA degree, Dad had retired, and he and Mom were living in Florida. I took a summer job as a super at Elmwood Apartments in my hometown. I had time to study and write essays. I wasn't much of a super. But at times, it was exciting. Like the time the woman got her toe caught in the hot water faucet of the bathtub in Apartment 103, and I had to get it loose.

Elaine Hopper, I remember her name, was kind of fat, but still, there were points of interest when I examined her naked body while I freed her toe. She clung to my leg when I was done, but I managed to get out of there.

I was reading chapter ten of *Elements of Physics* when Mary Lou entered my basement office below the apartments. I didn't recognize her voice when she cleared her throat several times to get my attention. I marked the page with a Greeley Office Supply paperweight and looked into her smiling eyes. She seemed taller, more assured than ever. God, she was beautiful. Later she insisted she might be beautiful in my eyes – she hoped she was – but that she was as common as your average movie star or fashion model. It was a few seconds before I realized the humor in her remark.

"Harold Weeks, as I live and breathe," she said.

The top of her partially unbuttoned sheer blouse stretched. It was even more impressive than the sweaters she used to wear.

"I saw the ad in the Daily News. I need an apartment. I suppose I'm too late."

I managed to stand and said, "There's only one."

She smiled. "One is all I want. May I see it?"

"How have you been, Mary Lou?"

"Fine, Harold, just fine. Except for my divorce. But even that was for the best. I've had it with living with my parents in Florida. I need a place of my own here."

I stumbled, getting around the desk, and led her to Apartment 103. Miss Hopper, the one with the caught toe, had moved out and left a mess behind.

"I haven't had a chance to clean yet. The previous occupant just moved out a couple of days ago."

"Harold, you've filled out. Not so skinny."

"So have you," I said. "I think you're the most beautiful woman in the world."

She smiled and shook her head slowly.

"Remember how you used to try to show off for me? It was so funny. You kept me laughing all the way through elementary and high school. I didn't understand what a compliment it was. Looking back, I think you were in love with me."

"I was. I am."

"Still?"

"Yes, still. I mean, well, I'm no good at this. I'm sorry."

"How much?"

"What?"

"How much rent for the apartment?"

"Oh," I managed to say.

I told her the monthly rent amount, and she said, "I'll take it if you'll help me clean it, wash my back when I call, and keep trying to impress me."

Desire took control of my brain. I bent to one knee, nearly lost my balance as it rested on the floor, and whispered, "Will you marry me?"

"Why, Harold. This is so sudden."

I feared she was making fun of me but blurted out, "Well, will you marry me?"

"Of course not. I'm just getting over divorcing Brad Thomas. You remember him. The jock. He ran off with a blonde, Elsie Goodwin. I don't think you knew her. At first, I was furious, but it was the best thing that ever happened to me. I'm glad he's gone."

I struggled to my feet. She smiled and shook her head.

"Let's get started," she said.

"I want to move in as soon as possible."

We hauled partially empty cereal boxes, some rags left in the closet, and a broken chair into the hallway. I swept the kitchen and living room floors. She spot-cleaned the carpet in the living room. I cleaned the bathroom.

As I scrubbed the tub, I imagined her in it and me washing her back. Of course, she didn't mean it, I told myself, but still . . .

"I'll be back tomorrow," she said. I nodded and watched as she left.

It all seems so long ago, in some ways, but in other ways, you know.

We live in a house on Elm Street now. Have for fifty years. She and our daughter, Eleanor, are talking in the living room.

"What's he doing now?" I heard Ellie say.

"He's trying to make soup. He loves to try to cook for me."

I stirred the bean soup. It smelled different. Probably too much spice again. She'd probably want to eat out again.

I didn't mind. I still liked showing off for her.

BONUS BABY
By **BOB LITER**

"I'm just naturally drawn to you, Amy, because of your 68% waist-to-hip ratio. Means you're fertile."

Barry Cartwright, the big lug, nursed a draft beer for half an hour in Central City's Lazy Hour Tavern before springing that statement on me. I moved behind the bar to the only other customer, an old guy named Armstrong, and served him his third glass of beer. He would down it soon and say goodnight.

Then, if Barry shut up, I could return to studying South American geography, a college course I thought would be a snap. No such luck. The professor, a geek named Omar Thomas, who always needed a shave and wore leather pants, expected his students to study. So that's what I was trying to do on this slow Monday night.

I mumbled to myself, "Montedeveo, capital of Uruguay, almost fifty percent of the nation's population. A modern metropolis with a historical old town. Surrounded by white sandy beaches. Highlights include Ciudad Vieja, Old Town, with its 18th-century buildings, bustling commercial activity, and its theaters, museums, and art galleries."

"How come you talk to yourself but won't talk to me?" Barry whined.

"I'm trying to study for a test." I looked over the rim of my glasses.

"I may have a job at the University of Illinois this fall if I want it," he said. "Where you going to school?"

"ICC, the junior college here."

I picked up his glass, wiped the bar with a soft white rag that was ready for the laundry, and said, "Won't the girls be thrilled! Especially, the ones that measure up to your fertility standards. I'm surprised you're interested in a female's pregnancy potential. You want to be a father?"

"Sure," he said, "eventually."

"Won't some girl be lucky?"

He sipped beer, gazed at me with deep blue eyes, and said, "Hey. Why be pissed at me? What did I ever do to you?"

"You insulted me, that's what. And, to make it worse, I bet you don't remember."

He put his elbow on the bar, rested his chin on his hand, and said, "Why would I insult you? When? I never insulted you."

"At the Century Movie House during the summer before you went away to college."

"Whatever I said, I'm sorry."

"It was a romantic movie, and you fell asleep."

"Hey, I remember now. I was tired. Stayed out too late the night before. Was so tired I couldn't sleep at home. That's why I was there. Wasn't like a date or anything. I just happened to sit beside you. How did I insult you?"

"You were such a big shot. Got a baseball scholarship to Illinois. I was thrilled to be sitting beside you. Next thing I know, you're snoring."

He moved his hand away from his chin and sipped more beer.

"A lot's happened since then," he said as he gazed right through my blouse.

I said, "To you. Not to me. I'm still stuck here trying to graduate so I can amount to something."

He lifted his face, straightened his shoulders, and said, "Looks to me like you amounted to something already. The hip, waist ratio for one thing."

He made me nervous like he did in high school during

assembly when he noticed I was looking at him. I turned to the sink and washed the beer glasses I'd already washed.

"Aren't bartenders supposed to talk to customers?"

I dried my hands and said, "What are your plans now that you blew out your arm?"

"You know about that?"

"Sure, everybody around here, that's half alive, knows about it. You get a million-dollar bonus for signing with the Cubs, work your way up to the majors, and your shoulder gives out after two wins. Doctors say you're through."

He looked down at the bar, drew a circle with his glass, and said, "It wasn't quite a million dollars. I didn't believe the doctors at first, but now I know I'll never be able to pitch in the majors again."

"A rotten break," I said. "But, I hear you've been bowling a ton of games at Crossroads. Doesn't that hurt your arm?"

"You seem to know a lot about me."

"I tend bar. Guys talk about sports. Besides, I like sports. Plan to be a sports reporter. Majoring in journalism."

He stretched his left arm across the bar. "Doesn't hurt except when I throw overhand. Bowling doesn't hurt. Different motion. Need to be able to repeat the same mechanics, though, to be successful in either sport. I'm gonna try the pro bowlers' tour."

"Anything to avoid work, huh."

I ran the soapy water out of the sink behind the bar, wiped things off, and said, "Well, it's time to close. Good luck on the tour."

He slid off the bar stool, stretched his arm again, and said, "I'll be back."

At the door, he turned and smiled.

I pretended I didn't notice.

He came back to the bar often that summer, mostly just an hour or so before closing. We talked when there was time. Despite all the guy's offers to buy him drinks, he didn't drink much.

I couldn't ignore him, even when I was busy. How can you

ignore a guy who has measured your pregnancy potential with his eyes and keeps checking to be sure he is right?

One night in the middle of August, he said, "I'll be watching the sports pages for your stories. I'm going to St. Louis to work with some pro bowlers; get ready for the tour."

A couple of days later, at Crossroads Lanes, I asked the manager, a guy named Kurt Weaver, about Barry Cartwright.

"I'm studying to be a sports reporter and plan to write an article about him," I said.

I asked Kurt how he spelled his last name, even though I knew. It's a trick I learned while working on my high school paper. Imply the name of the person you're questioning will be in the article, and they'll usually tell you what you want to know.

Kurt said, "Barry's good. Can string strikes here. Probably the best bowler in town. But he's going to see many different lane conditions on the tour. They dress them in different ways. What favors some guys is killing others. The best ones can adjust and in a hurry. And conditions change from one lane to the next during qualifying and match play."

I held up a hand to slow him down, caught up with my notes, and said, "Do you think he can make it?"

"Never know." He brushed a hand over his closely cropped hair and continued, "Nobody from around here ever has. Several have tried."

I gathered more information about Barry's baseball history from a couple of professional bowlers I contacted by email and wrote the article. I sent it to the local paper, the Gazette, and they printed it. No pay, though. They said they would print more of my stuff, maybe. I said, "No thanks." No pay, no play, that's my motto.

The tour opened the last week in September. I read the results on the Internet. In the first tournament, Barry finished 87th and failed to qualify for the finals. For the next three weeks, he also failed to qualify. Once he averaged 212 a game and missed qualifying by ten pins. After that, his name never appeared in any of the results.

I moped around campus, turned down several offers for dates from guys who may or may not have realized my pregnancy potential, and looked forward to graduation and the day I could go after stories, including whatever happened to Barry Cartwright.

Graduation ceremonies were in the last week in May. My parents came from Florida. Some aunts and uncles were there. Even my brother, the doctor from back east, came to see me get my diploma.

And I got a job as an intern sports reporter for the Chicago Times. I covered some crap assignments well enough to get assigned to write features about the University of Illinois football and basketball teams. I saw Barry one spring day as I hung around the athletic director's office, trying to find someone who knew about a change in the football team's schedule.

He smiled. Where had he been after giving me that come-on at the bar? I knew, of course, that it was nothing more than that. Just a come-on and only a halfhearted one at that. Still, I had been seeing his smile and his deep blue eyes in my sleep. I daydreamed about him coming to get me, about my pregnancy ratio, and how it was going to waste.

I'd even dated some guys, but it was no good.

"Hi," he said. Like he'd just seen me the day before.

I gulped and managed to say, "What are you doing here?"

"I'm the assistant baseball coach. Gonna teach these kids how not to ruin their arms."

"Too bad someone didn't teach you."

"They tried up in the bigs, but it was too late. How you been?"

"Fine. Just fine. And you?"

His skin was darker than I remembered it. But his blue eyes gazed at me in the same serious manner.

"Montevideo," he said.

"Montevideo?"

He recited the stuff I had mumbled in the bar that night that seemed so long ago.

"The part about the white beaches got me. After I flunked out on the bowling tour, I went there for a final fling. Layed around on the beaches for a month."

"What were you doing, checking the fertility ratios of the beach bunnies?"

"Yeah, that, and I did some thinking too. Decided to get on with my life. Gonna study more about coaching, maybe some other stuff. And start a family. I've been keeping track of your career."

My heart fluttered just a bit.

"Gee, won't some girl be lucky now that you've decided to start a family."

"Yeah, maybe. Let's go get something to eat and talk about it."

He was right about my fertility potential. We've been married for three years now and have created three wonderful children.

HOUSEKEEPING 101
By **BOB LITER**

His dark eyes glistened with concentration as he washed asparagus spears. One bare arm, rippling with muscles, stretched to retrieve a pan from the top shelf of the kitchen cabinet. Tight jeans outlined the length of his legs. His chest filled his short-sleeved shirt. Sweat beaded on his brow. He flipped a towel from a wall rack and wiped his tanned face. He folded it carefully and put it back. As he turned toward me, I put my hands on the table and pretended to look at them.

"May I get you another drink, Jan?" he asked.

"No thanks, not yet." I displayed my half-filled glass of white wine.

I never imagined when Roger Taylor invited me to dinner; he would cook it himself in his Good Housekeeping apartment. My name is Jan Cooper. I'm the receptionist at Finch-Taylor Insurance Agency in downtown Central City. Roger is the younger part of Finch-Taylor.

He placed a saucepan on the stove, melted two tablespoons of butter, added a bit of salt and two tablespoons of flour, and stirred.

"It's important to get the ingredients mixed well," he said, "but I'm sure you know that."

I nodded. He measured out two cups of milk and slowly poured it into the mixture, stirring all the while. He added a cup of shredded cheddar cheese and stirred until he was satisfied.

"The sauce is the thing," he said as he layered the asparagus and the sauce in a gleaming baking dish.

"Hope you like asparagus."

"I love asparagus," I said with my fingers crossed. I still clung to the idea that a lie didn't count if you crossed your fingers.

"I saw you in My Fair Lady."

"Really. That was two months ago?"

I was surprised. The local Theater Guild staged the play, and I had a small part. Roger and I see each other daily at work; this was the first time he mentioned it.

"You a member of the guild?" I asked.

"No, maybe I should support it. I just heard you were going to be in the play."

What to say? Should I ask him if he thought I was star material? Did he enjoy it?

Before I could decide, he said, "I thought your round face and cute figure were just right for that racing scene. The big floppy hat and the way you paraded around the stage was something I'll remember."

"Thank you," I managed. My round face. Cherubic, my mother called it.

The evening was pleasant enough. We listened to some classy jazz, talked about work, and drank wine. I was nervous about that. Scared I might spill some on the light blue cushioned chair on which I was sitting.

After we ate, we washed and dried the dishes. He put them away carefully and checked each cupboard before he closed the door.

He drove me home and kissed me at the side of his car when I refused his offer to see me to the door. My building was nice enough, all brick and glass, the hallways were clean, and even the elevator was neat. I opened the door to my apartment, Number 310, and stumbled over a plastic sack I should have picked up after I dropped it a few days before. I stooped, picked it up, gathered the newspaper pages on the floor and couch, and piled them on the kitchen table beside the breakfast dishes.

The next morning, before I went to work, I picked up the sweater hanging on the kitchen chair, the pair of shoes in the corner, and the blouse I had planned to wash two days before. I'd do the dirty dishes that night when I got home from work, maybe. The wadded-up editorial page of the local newspaper was still in the sink where I'd thrown it after reading that the mayor was right when he insisted we didn't need any more street sweepers. He should drive down my street and see all the leaves.

Three days later, on a Friday after he had been out of the office most of the time, Roger asked me to go for a picnic. He followed me outside, where October skies leaked raindrops on my head.

He must have read my mind. "Supposed to be sunny tomorrow," he said.

"I haven't been on a picnic in years," I said. "I'd love to."

I spent half a week's salary on a pair of designer blue jeans, new loafers, and a sweatshirt that advertised the Saint Louis Cardinals. I thought about that on the way home. Why did I buy that sweatshirt? I don't like baseball. Did he? I had no idea. Just another dumb thing I did. Like the baseball cap I wore to the picnic. It was one my brother left behind.

It did keep the rain out of my eyes. The "sunny tomorrow" prediction turned out to be as wrong as the whole date. We got soaked, the sandwiches were soggy, and my feet hurt. We walked to the edge of a lake, about two blocks from the car, when the sky dropped its load on us.

He drove to my building and pouted when I refused to let him come in. With unwashed breakfast dishes in the sink and clothes from the day before strewn on the living room couch and floor, there was no way he was going to get inside.

The next day, or maybe it was two days later, I scrubbed the kitchen floor, emptied the garbage, ran the vacuum on the living room carpet, hung up my clean clothes, and put the dirty stuff in a hamper I had to go out and buy, and waited.

He was frequently in and out of the office, nodded at me when he passed my desk, but didn't stop and talk like before. And he didn't ask me out on a date. I was seriously thinking of inviting him to eat with me at a nearby restaurant -- my turn to treat, I would say -- but abandoned the idea. I could see no future for Mr. Clean and me, even if he was the hunkiest guy I'd ever seen, and I was ready to be domesticated.

A week later, he stopped at my desk and said, "Jan, I'm, well, that is, you see, I enjoyed that night when I cooked supper for you so much; could I do it again?

"Do you know how to make something besides that asparagus thing?" I asked as if that made any difference.

"Sure, how about vegetable soup?"

I laughed. This guy would be fixing something fancier than vegetable soup, wouldn't he?

I hesitated for just a moment and said, "Yeah, I guess. Why not?"

We closed the office that night, and he escorted me to his shiny new black BMW. I enjoyed the comfort of the passenger seat so much that I didn't notice he was going away from his apartment to another part of town. He parked behind Excel Arms, a large, tall building with parking space for maybe fifty cars, each space marked with a name.

"Why are we here?" I asked. Was he trying to pull something, like my leg?

"I live here," he said. "Got a nice view of Bradley Park."

Three people, a woman wearing glasses lodged on an upturned nose, a man carrying a briefcase, and a teenager with earphones glued to his head, joined us in the elevator. We were the first to get off on the fourth floor, and I followed him to his apartment, Four Zero Nine. The gold letters on the door were spelled out.

"But I thought . . ."

"Oh, you mean the other apartment. That's my mother's. She was visiting my sister. Let me use it, but made me promise not to make a mess. She's a clean freak."

We entered a large living room. Roger ducked behind a three-cushion couch and came up with a sweatshirt, a pair of smelly socks, and one running shoe. He tossed them into the bedroom off to the side and closed the door.

"Come look at the view," he said.

I followed him into the kitchen and noted several dirty dishes in the sink. We stood behind a blond kitchen table cluttered with magazines, his arm around my shoulder. The park stretched out before us. Multicolored leaves carpeted the ground. The surface of a small lake glistened in the twilight. I leaned against him, content to stand there forever.

"I'm starving. I'll bet you are. Can you wait until I get something delivered? Pizza, maybe?"

"Pizza? I came here expecting a kitchen demonstration. Like on television. Like last time."

"Were you impressed? I practiced that recipe for a week. I don't know how to cook anything else."

"Pizza will be fine," I said.

While we waited for the pizza, I talked him into drying while I washed the dirty dishes. Someone had to teach him how not to be a slob.

THE SNOWSTORM
By **BOB LITER**

That summer, people in Fork were still talking about the February snowstorm. Thirty inches of the stuff dumped on the town in half a day.

All who could get away attended the July 15 hearing in the bare room with the fold-down chairs in the county courthouse at Jayson.

Judge Homer Hopp, waving a giant gavel above his bald head, shushed everyone and said, "This is not a circus. If you people don't quiet down, I'll clear the room."

A court bailiff, wearing multicolored suspenders to hold up too-large pants, swore in Buford Dewitt as he sat in the witness chair beside the judge. Dewitt's fat legs didn't reach the floor, and his face was redder than usual.

The judge said, "Now I understand, Mr., er, Dewitt, that you've filed these assault charges.

"Buford Dewitt. That is correct, your honor."

Buford looked at his wife, Hester, who sat in the front row. When people behind her complained, Hester removed her wide-brimmed hat with a bunch of fake grapes.

"Tell me why you filed these charges," the judge said.

Buford hemmed a little, hawed a little, and after getting a stern look from Hester, said, "Well, your honor, he knocked me down. When I tried to get up, he knocked me down again. Then he knocked my wife down. Into the snow drift."

The judge shuffled some papers and said, "Mr., what is it, Best? Yes, Mr. Best, what about that?"

Dan Best was sworn in after Buford left the witness chair.

"I didn't knock him or Hester down. I shoved 'em. They just fell into the snow drift. I shoved Buford back down when he tried to get up because I was tired of him taking swings at me. Hester socked me with her purse."

"How tall are you, Mr. Best?" the judge asked.

"About six foot two," Dan said.

"How tall is Mr. Dewitt?"

"Don't know."

"Well," the judge said, "I can see he's not much more than five feet. As I understand it, this happened in Mr. Dewitt's driveway. Is that correct?"

"Yes," Dan said.

"What were you doing there?"

"I was plowing snow onto the entrance of his drive."

"Why were you doing that, Mr. Best?"

Dan faced the judge. He ran a big hand through his short-cropped hair.

"It's a long story," Dan said.

The judge stood and faced Dan.

"I don't care; I want to know why you were blocking Mr. Dewitt's drive."

"He's one of our councilmen."

"Fork has councilmen?"

"Yes, three."

"So?"

Dan sat down. The judge sat down.

"We elected 'em several years ago. Ollie's the mayor; Buford Dewitt is the street commissioner, and Gregory Lancaster collects the garbage."

"Yes, yes, go on."

Dan fidgeted in the witness chair.

"Well, you see, we had this snowstorm last February. Big

one. Buford rents John Turner's tractor, the one with the plow attachment, and plows our streets. That's his job. Gets paid fifty dollars when he has to plow. The first time he ever had to work for it."

The judge stood up, shook his left leg, sat down again, and said, "Get to the point."

"Buford plows his own street, College Street, first," Dan said.

"College Street? I didn't know you had a college in Fork." the judge said.

"We don't. That's just the street's name."

"So?"

"Buford plowed his own street first, comes back and clears the plowed snow from his driveway entrance, then goes about the rest of the town plowing the streets and blocking everyone else's driveway."

Buford stood beside Hester and said, "I can explain that, your honor."

"Explain it," the judge said.

"There's no way I could have gotten all the streets plowed if I stopped to clear every driveway. I cleared mine because Hester, well, she said I had to because of the historical club meeting."

"And because of this, you, Mr. Best, plowed what was it, four feet of snow back into Mr. Dewitt's drive? Is that correct?"

"Correct, your honor," Buford said.

"I was asking Mr. Best."

"Correct, your honor," Dan said, mimicking Buford.

The judge turned to the bailiff and said, "We have several more cases scheduled this morning, don't we?"

"Yes, judge, we do."

"Cases like this have overloaded my court and kept me from playing golf for a week. Case dismissed."

"Now, all you Forkers, go home and be nice to each other."

THE WAY THE COOKIE CRUMBLES

A Nick Bancroft Mystery
By **BOB LITER**

Maggie Atley, my apartment mate at the time, came into the kitchen, sat across from me at the fold-down table, and said, "There was a phone call for you while you were out. A Raymond Anders. Says he wants you to find out who's crushing the cookies Heartland Distributing Company displays in Grunder's Grocery Store. I told him you'd give him a call as soon as you got back." She smiled. I threatened to crumble her cookie. "Nick, you need the money."

My name is Nick Bancroft. I'm a freelance reporter and sometimes a private investigator. I was investigating a murder, a rare thing in Central City, and didn't much care about crumbled cookies. However, she was right about my finances. She left for her library job after making a fresh pot of coffee. I fetched a cup, looked at the Springfield phone number she had written large enough so I couldn't miss it, and dialed.

"This is the strangest thing, Mr. Bancroft," Anders said after we got past the introductions. "Someone is deliberately destroying our products after we deliver them to the grocery store there. Nowhere else. Just in Central City. This person somehow crushes the bags of cookies without getting caught. No one will buy them, of course. We're losing money, and it's got to be hurting our reputation. We have always sold lots of cookies in Grunder's Grocery Store."

"Have you been to the police?"

"No, we don't want that, not yet anyway. Don't want publicity. If this got in your local paper, it would be a joke. Hurt our business even more."

"Look, Mr. Anders, I'm sorry. I'm working on a murder case that's taking up all my time. I don't think I have time for cookie crushers."

"We thought it would be cheaper to hire you than to send a detective up there from here. We'd pay you five hundred dollars if you bring this nonsense to a halt. We don't even want to prosecute; too much publicity."

"Well," I said. "I'll see if I can work it in. Get back to you in a day or two." I wondered why anyone would keep crumbling those particular cookies. Maybe teenagers. They might think it's funny. I was talking to myself again.

I finished my coffee and headed for Grunder's. Getting my mind off the murder investigation temporarily might jab my subconscious into thinking of something. Grunder's is several blocks west of my place, on Lexington Avenue. It's the best grocery store in Central City, Maggie says.

I pushed a cart at the store and wandered from one aisle to the other, watching. I watched women of all shapes and sizes, with children and without. I watched men, usually older. It was easy to imitate them. Most, apparently, had nothing better to do than pick up items, read the small print, and return them to the shelf. A young professional woman raced through the store, grabbed groceries she'd apparently already decided to buy, and went past me like an ill wind.

I moseyed down wide aisles, past islands of stacked cans or boxes, looked at candy, cakes, and pies, and caught whiffs of enticing smells. My nose directed me to a corner away from the entrance where all sorts of delicious-looking prepared foods were offered for sale. It reminded me of a seed catalog where every flower looked perfect. I figured this must be the picture women have in mind when they fuss over how food looks on their tables.

I followed, at a distance, two teenage boys who should have been in school. They stopped at the candy aisle, fingered several packages of pimple producers, and selected a bag of chocolate kisses. They checked out with several over-the-shoulder glances my way.

I was approaching the cookie aisle when the store manager, Charlie Booker, spotted me. I'd known him casually for a couple of years. Did a story on his yard once. He plowed the whole thing and grew county-fair prize vegetables and flowers. You'd think a guy who raised food and sold food would be fat, or at least large, but Charlie was a thin, short, nervous guy with uneven teeth.

"You here to catch our cookie cruncher, or are you just shopping?" he asked. "They told me you might look into it. Here's the latest batch of crunched cookies. I left them on the shelf so you can see what's happening. Look at them. Why would anyone keep doing this? I think it's kids, but I can't catch 'em."

There were perhaps twenty bags of Heartland Cookies, each wrinkled and squashed. As if a child who couldn't get the packages open had smashed the contents out of frustration. "Let's go to your office. I'd like to look at your employee records. You do have background information on all of them, don't you?"

"Sure, more on some than others. The kids, the baggers, we don't have that much on some. They quit before we get time to complete their records."

I glanced through the records Booker had placed on a desk he had cleared off. It was as exciting as counting money, someone else's. I had asked for only last year's records and was checking the last of them without seeing anything interesting. Then I noted the Roger Warner file. He worked in produce and was a retired Heartland truck driver. He worked nights - the store was opened 24 hours a day, every day - and lived in Central City.

I copied the address and drove to his house, only a couple more blocks on Lexington and two blocks to the left on Bigelow.

It was a small white house set farther from the street than the rest. Figuring he was probably asleep since he worked nights, I pounded on the door like a stormtrooper.

He appeared eventually, his eyes bleary, his face partially covered by a two-day growth of gray whiskers. He wore a terry cloth robe that needed washing. I opened the screen door and pushed past him. "What the hell," he grumbled as he stepped back and looked at me with suddenly alert eyes.

"I'm here about the cookies. No sense in denying it. We have surveillance photos. You tell me what this is all about now, or you can do it later at the police station." He backed away and sank into a worn couch. He put his hands to his face and moaned.

"Well?" I said.

"It's my pension. I drove for Heartland for twenty years. Now they're cheating me out of my pension. Had to take that job at the grocery store. The bastards. I knew it was stupid, crushing their damned cookies. But I had to get back at them somehow. Now I'm the one who's going to get it in the ass again. Oh, hell. Give me a chance to get dressed. I'll go with you."

I sat on the couch beside him. "You can relax. You're right. It was stupid. You promise me this cookie crunching will stop. Nobody needs to know it was you. One more crunch, though, and you're in trouble."

He started to explain how the company had fired him just before he would be eligible to collect his pension. I stopped him. There was nothing I could do about that.

At my office, I called Booker and told him to remove the crunched cookies and that the case had been solved. He wanted details. I didn't give any. Heartland wanted details, also. I told them I had solved the case, there would be no more cookie crunching, and they could send me the five-hundred dollars in a week or when they were convinced the problem had been solved. The guy I was talking to, a vice president, reluctantly agreed. I breathed a sigh of relief. I would soon be solvent again.

ELEMENTARY

A Nick Bancroft Mystery
By **BOB LITER**

Nick Bancroft sat at the kitchen table across from me and said, "Remember Tom Bradford? His wife's missing, and police think he killed her. I'm going to Springfield tonight to talk to him. He says she's hiding, and he has to find her."

My name is Maggie Atley. I'm a librarian with two adult sons, an ex-husband who ignores me, and Mr. private detective Bancroft, who doesn't ignore me. But he sometimes annoys me because he thinks he's so smart.

"Take me with you," I said.

"He invited me to dinner. He didn't invite you."

"But you're going to. Invite me to dinner. I'll be quiet as a mouse."

"Sure you will."

I kissed Nick on the forehead and said, "I was forced, when you and Tom talked sports, to listen to his wife, Candy, tell me what a wonderful model she was. What a glamorous life she led before she married Tom. And I suffered from envying her slim frame. It reminded me that my modeling days were over."

"Were you a model?"

"No. Why do the police think he killed her?"

Nick stood and said, "Do whatever you do to get ready. I'm leaving in ten minutes."

Twenty minutes later, I was ready. Nick growled. We'd be late for his appointment, and he said, when I asked him again, "Police think Tom killed her because they found a smear of her blood in the bathtub and learned that Tom's got a mistress. According to her sister, Candy, his wife has been missing for three weeks."

Nick was silent the rest of the way to Springfield. I pretended to sleep. I intended to keep out of it; I really did.

At Eddie's, a swank restaurant not far from the classy neighborhood where Tom lived, a young thing named Naomi accompanied Tom. Nick, Naomi, and Tom ordered steaks plus trimmings. I had a salad.

"My wife's hiding out to embarrass me," Tom said. "I asked for a divorce, and she went berserk. She admitted marrying me for security and said she'd never give me a divorce. In comparison, Naomi is a loving woman."

He looked at the young thing. She smiled demurely.

"Candy didn't want anything to do with me once we were married," he said.

I managed to stay out of the conversation during the rest of the meal. When the table was cleared, Nick said, "I'll want to go to your house; look around."

"Sure," Tom said. "Police have already done that. Maybe you'll see something they didn't."

The two-story house, on the corner of Lexington and California, featured fancy columns on either side of the front door. The yard, what I could see of it, was covered with fall leaves.

Tom and Naomi sat at an oak dining room table, sipping bourbon, as Nick wandered around doing his investigative thing. I was directed upstairs when I asked about the location of the bathroom.

"There's one off the master bedroom," Tom said. "I promised police I wouldn't use the one down here."

"They put that awful yellow tape across the door," Naomi said. It was the first time I'd heard her voice except for the introductions at the restaurant.

Nick had already been upstairs and was in the kitchen.

I did use the bathroom, but the real reason I was there was to look around. I noted the plush carpeting and the canopied bed with the pastel bedding. I thought of Tom's wife's stories about living with her mother in a dirty cabin on Lake Oxford north of Chicago after her father died.

"Mother still owns it, but since she remarried, we've never gone back," Candy had said.

I examined her giant closet, a sliding door affair. It was close to full. There were no casual clothes there, but then I'd never seen Candy wear anything casual. I checked the large cabinet in the bathroom. Tom's shaving gear and stuff were on one side. The other side was empty.

I sat on the edge of the bed. Something wasn't right. Something I'd seen? Something I hadn't seen? Nick appeared in the doorway and leaned against it like a long-legged movie cowboy who had just caught the villain. He said, "I knew you'd stick your nose in."

"Can I help it if I had to go to the bathroom?"

"Of course not. Is that why you're sitting on the bed looking like you can't remember how."

I got up, pushed him away from the door, and headed downstairs. I stopped halfway down. *I knew*. He ran into my behind. I turned and took him in my arms. I kissed him long and gently.

"What's going on with you two? Can't you wait 'til you get home?" Tom said from below.

I said, "Candy is hiding out at that cabin her mother owns."

"What cabin? Does her mother own a cabin? Do you know where it is?" Nick asked.

Tom stood and said, "Yeah, she owns a cabin. It's just outside of Oxford."

"What makes you think she's there, Maggie?"

"Just have the police check," I said.

I worried I'd made a fool of myself all the way home and into the following afternoon. What about the blood in the bathtub? Maybe she cut herself shaving her legs and just smeared it there.

Finally, Tom called and said the police found her at the cabin, alive and well.

"How did you know?" Tom asked.

"Her cosmetics were missing," I said.

Later, when Nick got home, he asked me the same thing.

After sitting on his lap at the kitchen table, I patted his head and said, "Her face was gone. If Tom had killed her, her face would still be there."

"What the devil does that mean?"

"It's just elementary, my dear Watson."

THE CON GAME
A Nick Bancroft Mystery
By **BOB LITER**

I slouched on a chair in The Hole in the Wall, a small, dimly lit joint with a bar beyond mismatched tables and chairs. A blonde waitress, with dark-haired roots and all, strolled to my table and said, "What would you like?"

"What I would like is you," I said, "but for now, I'll take a shot of Lord Calvert and a glass of beer."

She smiled, returned to the bar, held an animated conversation with the bartender, a husky bald guy who wore red suspenders, and returned with the order.

Three days later, after I'd stopped by every afternoon, Roxie -- her name was embroidered on her blouse -- got really friendly. She hitched up her brassiere and called me Jay. I'd told her my name was Jay Winthrop.

While she got my usual order, I adjusted my Armani shirt and Gleason slacks and made sure my scuffed loafers were out of sight. She returned and placed the order in front of me, offering me a close, revealing view of her chest.

"My feet hurt," she said. "They always hurt this time of day."

"Sit down, Roxie," I said.

"Would you mind, Jay? I won't stay long."

I pushed the glass of beer her way. "Have some if you want."

It was time to make my move.

"I'm staying at the Roosevelt. It's a cab trip away. Been working on this business deal for three days now. Wish I had a closer place to take an afternoon nap," I said.

She removed a shoe, wiggled her foot, replaced the shoe, and said, "You could flop at my place. I live above this joint. Good enough to catch a nap if you want."

I sipped whiskey, looked over the rim of the glass, and said, "Gee, that's awfully nice of you. If I weren't intruding, I'd go up there after I finish this drink and sleep."

"Well, why not?" She removed the other shoe, wiggled her toes, replaced the shoe, and said, "Soon as you're ready."

"Can you just leave?"

She nodded toward the bartender and said, "He can wait on anyone that comes in while I'm gone. Do him good to get off his duff."

Her round bottom bobbed as she climbed the stairs ahead of me. Her living room included a couch, a couple of chairs, and a television set. The window looked out on a roof across the way and an alley below. The cluttered kitchen had worn oil paper on the counter and a rusty sink.

"The bedroom's in here," she said.

An ashtray on the dresser was nearly overflowing with cigarette butts.

"If I didn't have to work, I wouldn't mind joining you."

I put my coat on the back of the nearest chair and lay on the bed. She hesitated and then lay close beside me. She kissed me. She put her arm around my shoulder, moved closer, and kissed me again.

"Well, that's all I can do for you now. I've got to get back to work."

An hour later, I went back to the bar, ordered a beer, gulped it, smiled at her, and said, "I'll be back tomorrow for sure."

I returned the next afternoon, sat at my usual table, and ordered a glass of beer. Roxie seemed nervous. The bartender brought the beer and a manila envelope and sat across from me.

"You know Roxie's my wife?" he asked.

"Yeah, I figured that's how it was, or at least that's what you'd claim. Nothing serious happened between us if that's what you're worried about."

"You're the one who ought to be worried. Look at these. And don't get any ideas. I've got the negatives."

He pulled three eight-by-ten photos from the envelope and flipped them across the table. They showed Roxie and me in bed kissing.

I glanced at them and said, "All we did was kiss."

He pointed at me and said, "Look, Mr... Nobody fools with my wife. You pay, or I'll find out where you live, give the pictures to your wife, maybe your boss, too. I can find out where you work, Mr. Winthrop."

"What makes you think I'm married?"

He grinned.

"You ain't too smart, wearing a wedding ring when you plan to fool around."

Roxie was behind the bar. She glanced at me and glanced away.

"So, what do you want me to do?" I asked as if I didn't know.

"You pay me ten thousand dollars. I give you the photos and negatives," he said.

"Ha. Where am I gonna get ten thousand dollars? Think I carry that kinda money around with me?"

He scrapped the chair on the floor as he stood and said, "You be back here tomorrow with the money, or I start looking for your wife or anybody else who would be interested."

"Damn," I said. "Look at all the money I spent in here. Just trying to relax after a big deal, and you pull this. I have been set up. Damn you and your wife."

"That's right, Mr. Winthrop, you've been set up. You should know better."

I pushed myself away from the table, stood, scowled at him, and said, "I'll be back tomorrow."

The next afternoon Roxie didn't seem to be around. The bartender marched to my table with his thumbs on his suspenders. I ordered a glass of beer.

He poured the beer from the customer side of the bar, placed it in front of me, and said, "Got the money?"

I reached into my inside coat pocket and handed him a tape recording.

"What's this crap?" he said.

"You listen to that. You'll hear a guy sounds just like you trying to extort me."

"But I got the pictures. I'll expose you if you don't pay up."

"No, you won't. Not unless you're stupider than you look."

He snapped one of his suspenders against his chest and said, "Who are you?"

"My real name's Nick Bancroft. One of your blackmailed suckers hired me. Never mind which one. If you continue to squeeze him, I'll turn a copy of the tape over to the police." Roxie came down the stairs. I waved at her as I left and headed back to the quieter life.

THE ROOT OF THE MATTER

A Nick Bancroft Mystery
By **BOB LITER**

I sat at the bar in Otto's Tavern on Waters Street, reading the Central City Press sports page. Otto lowered his old bones to the worn, cushioned chair behind the bar. He commented occasionally on the news in the front section of the newspaper. I ignored him.

A woman wearing a floppy hat opened the front door, hesitated, allowed the morning sunlight to actually enter the place, and said in a voice that soothed and caressed, "Is Nick Bancroft here?"

That's me. I'm Central City's only freelance reporter and private investigator. I noted the curve of her hips, the classy cut of a well-fitted sky-blue suit jacket, and long, shapely legs extending from a short dark blue skirt. She carried a small blue purse.

Still, I hesitated to answer in case she was a bill collector. She said, "Well, surely the question is not that difficult for you two... gentlemen."

"I'm Nick Bancroft," I said.

"Could I tear you away from all this and go back to your office long enough to discuss business?"

The woman turned and left. I followed in the wake of her strides as we crossed Elmore street, went up the creaking wooden stairs, past the Ballard Inc. office on the second floor, and up to my third-floor place.

The notice informing potential customers I could be found at Otto's had been taped to the door. Now it lay crumpled on the floor.

My office housed a worn, oversized wooden desk with drawers that stuck, a swivel chair that didn't always swivel, and some battered filing cabinets. In front of the desk was a wooden chair for the occasional visitor. A radio with a cracked plastic case sat on the window ledge beside an ancient air-conditioner. The window, when it was clean, overlooked the back parking lot. My one-room living quarters adjoined the office. The rest of the third floor housed cobwebs and dust.

I settled behind the desk. After looking at the "guest" chair, the woman rejected my offer to sit. She removed her hat. I stared at her sensuous lips, green eyes, and abundant red hair.

I'm Cynthia Crawford," she announced. "My mother is Mrs. Norville Mortin. She's been missing for six weeks. Her husband claims he doesn't know where she is. I think he murdered her for her money. All I have is six hundred dollars. I'll pay you that if you find out what happened to her."

Norville Mortin. He lived in the spacious house at the north edge of Central City's extended boundaries.

I learned Mortin was a retired Springfield stock broker when I did a story on him for the Chicago Times.

"Have you reported this to the police?"

"Of course. They haven't found anything. Mortin claims she just left. Says she didn't tell him where she was going. I've checked with her sister in Florida and everyone else I can think of. No one has heard from her."

I studied her face. She turned away from my gaze.

"Is Mr. Mortin your father?"

"No, stepfather. I hate him."

"Why?"

"First of all, he married my mother for her money. She inherited a bundle when my father died. And the bastard tried to get in my pants more than once."

"Are you married?"

"Was once," she said. "What's that got to do with anything?"

"If I take the case, I'll have to have a retainer."

She removed her gloves one slim finger at a time.

"I'll write you a check for three hundred dollars for now," she said.

"That'll be fine," I said. She wrote the check and handed it to me.

"Do you have a photo of your mother?"

She riffled through her purse and produced a billfold photo of an older woman who didn't look like her at all.

"I'll give it a try," I said, "but I'm not sure I can do much of anything. Missing persons. Sometimes we never find out if it's because of foul play, or the person just wanted to get away from it all."

She stood, adjusted her skirt, and said, "My mother wasn't happy in her marriage to that rat. But she would never leave without letting me know where she was."

At the police station, Detective Andrew Brown, my main information source there, said, "We never found a trace of her. Her Mercedes is missing. Could have just taken off. Maybe we'll never know."

"I've been hired to find her. Her daughter thinks Mortin killed her for her money."

"Yeah, I know. Talked to her several times. Really wanted to help but couldn't get anywhere. Nice looker."

I left Brown and admired the rolling hills of the Mortin estate as I drove my '82 Escort up the winding drive to the parking area in front of the house. As I climbed out of the car, a large black dog galloped toward me. Its bark sent shivers down my spine despite the warm summer weather.

"Nice doggy," I said a couple of times without conviction. A man ran from behind the house and shouted, "Sit, Alexander, sit."

The dog skidded to a stop and sat before me like a wet-tongued statue.

"He probably won't bite you, but he jumps on people, scares the shit out of 'em."

"He didn't have to jump on me to do that," I said, still eyeing the dog as it eyed me.

"I'm busy out back mowing the grass. What do you want?"

Mortin hadn't changed much since I interviewed him a couple of years earlier. His forehead had receded a little more, perhaps. The beginning of a full beard covered part of his thin face. He wore blue jeans, a T-shirt, and running shoes. The last time I'd seen him, he was elegant in a silk suit.

"I'm here to ask some questions about your missing wife," I said.

"She's missing all right. Just up and left. I suppose her daughter hired you. Is that it?"

He turned and walked toward the side of the house where he had first appeared.

"Don't worry about the dog. He won't bother you now. Come, Alexander."

The dog bounded away. I followed without bounding.

The half-acre yard behind the house was edged with flower beds. Many flowers I couldn't identify bloomed in profusion even though weeds grew among them. The largest and most colorful red and pink roses I'd ever seen dominated one area. A riding mower was parked near the left edge of the yard.

"I've got nothing more to say. You'll have to excuse me; I want to get this grass mowed before the sun gets too hot."

"Your wife must have taken care of the flower beds," I said.

He seated himself on the mower and started it. He drove it to the end of the grass where a cornfield bordered the yard, turned, and headed back toward me.

"Just one more question," I shouted as he approached.

He shut off the mower and said, "One more. That's all."

"Why are the roses in that one bed growing so much taller than those in the other beds?"

I pointed to the lush roses and the competing weeds. His face turned red. He pulled a handkerchief from his hip pocket and wiped his brow. He stuffed the handkerchief back in his pocket, stared at me with menace in his eyes, and said, "That's your question? You stopped me for that? I don't know anything about the damned flowers. That was my wife's business."

He started the mower again, turned it near my feet, and headed to the far end of the yard.

I returned to the police station and Brown's office. He concentrated on papers from a file folder on his desk and ignored me. I sat and waited patiently. I was thinking of leaving, not so sure by then that I wanted to say what I had planned. It would make me look like a fool if I was wrong.

He pushed the papers aside, lit a half-smoked cigar he pulled from his top desk drawer, and said, "So?"

"I got an idea where maybe you can find the body of Mrs. Mortin."

"So?"

"Don't laugh. I think he buried her in a flower bed."

He moved his swivel chair back, put his feet on the desk, stretched his arms, and said, "And how did you deduce this, Sherlock?"

I squirmed in the chair. "The roses and weeds in a particular spot are lusher and taller than any of the others."

He smiled at me like a parent amused at a small child.

"You think the rotting body under those plants is supplying fertilizer, thus causing the plants to excel. Is that right?"

"Yeah, that's what I thought. Maybe it's a dumb idea."

"That big dog he's got. Maybe that's where it shits."

"That could be it," I said.

"Well, as dumb as cops are, sometimes we do look around. We examined the yard. Didn't see any suspicious dirt. The flowers were pretty well through for the season. I remember a compost pile on the left side of the yard. We had no reason to dig up his yard."

"Well, it was just an idea. The roses are on the left side of the yard. I didn't see any compost pile," I said.

A week later, Cynthia Crawford came into my office about an hour before noon. I didn't manage to get my feet off the desk before she saw them. I wondered if she realized I had been asleep.

She glanced at me, at the splendor of my office, and said, "I didn't really expect results, but you were all I could afford."

I figured she was going to ask for her retainer back. Maybe I should have returned it. I really hadn't done much. Missing persons' cases are tough. She sat on the chair in front of my desk, pulled her checkbook from a monster purse, and filled out a check. She handed it to me. It was for three hundred dollars."

"What's this for?"

"It's what I promised. I was hoping you'd find my mother alive, but at least you found her."

"I did?"

"That policeman, Mr. Brown, told me how they managed to get a search warrant after you told them where to find the remains of her body."

She wiped a tear from her eye and said, "I had my cry on the way here. At least this brings the thing to closure, and the cop assured me Mortin will stand trial."

"I'm sorry it had to end this way," I said after I regained my ability to speak.

I deposited the two checks in my depleted bank account the next day and left the bank feeling lousy. I'd read about the arrest of Norville Mortin and the filing of murder charges against him. I was surprised when he found me at Otto's a few days later.

"You dirty bastard," he said as he plowed up to the bar like a ship in a windstorm.

"I thought they arrested you," I managed to say.

"I'm out on bail. They're going to hang my ass because of you. Did that damned bitch tell you where she buried the body? Are you in on this with her? Gonna get your cut?"

"Now, wait a minute. Are you saying Cynthia killed her mother? And buried her in your flower bed?"

"That's what I'm saying, and I want to hire you to prove it."

"I'm not sure I believe you."

"You will take the money, won't you, and look into it?"

He offered a sum of money, and I didn't resist, but I could never find evidence that Cynthia did it. He told me to keep the money after they convicted him of murdering his wife. I still sometimes wonder if what he said was true. And I almost feel guilty about keeping Mortin's money.

NOW I GET IT

A Nick Bancroft Mystery
By **BOB LITER**

I was surprised that Sunday when Maggie flicked her tongue in my ear. She had stayed on her side of the bed for a week, discouraging me from joining her. What had been wrong? Did I forget her birthday? No, it wasn't for a month or two; I was almost sure. Maybe it was because I went to Chicago for a ball game with some guys and didn't invite her.

I lifted my head from the pillow. Morning sunlight filtered through the fluttering curtains.

"What time is it?"

"Almost seven," she said.

She dug an elbow into the mattress, propped her chin on her hand, and said, "What attracted you? Why are you still attracted? You are still attracted to me, aren't you?"

I stretched, settled back into a sleep position, and mumbled, "Are these trick questions?"

She flipped the sheet to the foot of the bed, tickled my bare chest by swishing her hair across it, brushed her lips on my skin, and said, "Not trick questions."

Was this an opportunity? I rubbed my nose into her shoulder and caught a whiff of apple shampoo. She didn't pull away. I gently slapped her sweet ass and said, "You're female."

"I understand that part, but why me?"

I sat up and tried to kiss her. She dodged away, laughed music into the room, a lonely place before her, and said, "C'mon, Nick. I'm serious."

She rested her head on my stomach and blew warm air toward my most sensitive area.

I caught my breath and said, "You had that all-knowing smile that suggested you knew I was intent on getting into your pants, so to speak, and yet you didn't pretend to be offended."

"Is that all?"

"I like the way, when I was allowed to caress them with my mouth, I like the way your nipples rise to the occasion."

She slapped my belly gently, moved her head, kissed my ear again, and whispered, "Tell me more, big boy."

I pressed my lips into a breast, inhaled the smell of her, and mumbled into her chest, "Your breasts are just the right size. So firm. They fit my mouth just about perfectly."

To prove it, I surrounded as much of one as possible with my lips. She pressed my nose into her chest and said, "And."

I reached down, rubbed the inside of her left leg well above the knee, and said, "Your legs. I like the firm muscles of your thighs, the slender beauty of your ankles, and the earthiness of your bare feet."

She rubbed her chest against mine and said, "This stuff is nice, but it's all physical."

I slapped her behind and said, "Your ass. I like how you tighten the muscles and let them go soft when I caress them."

She kissed me here and there and said, "Very nice again, but still only physical."

"Your eyes." I pushed my nose against hers. My eyes crossed.

"Still physical," she said.

"How about love. That's not physical. I love how you inspire the kids at the library when you read to them and how you make me a better person when I'm with you."

She covered my lower half, part of which was putting on a display, and said, "Very nice. Even the last part, which you picked up from a Jack Nicholson movie. You know, the one with Helen

Hunt. I wanted to see how far you'd go to avoid taking me to the band concert."

Damn, she never forgets. All the stuff I said was true, but ordinarily, I wouldn't talk about it. I was trying to soft-soap her to get out of the band concert thing. I wanted to watch the Chicago Bears exhibition game on television that night. She probably knew that, too.

"Are you sure I promised?"

The truth is I did. I guess it's a promise even if you make it under pressure and hope it will be forgotten.

Maggie said, "C'mon, Nick, the outdoor concert season is almost over."

She wiped an imaginary tear from under her right eye and said, "Please."

"I've got to run an errand."

"An errand? It better not keep you from taking me to the concert."

She frowned and tried to look fierce. Her eyelids closed partially, and her mouth turned down. But her eyes sparkled, and her lips curled up into a smile.

"It won't take long," I said.

"Then you'll take me along, won't you?"

My name is Nick Bancroft. In my hometown, Central City, Illinois, I squeeze out a living as a freelance reporter and private investigator.

She rolled out of bed and stretched. Light from the window cast breast shadows across her chest. The light emphasized the slight arch of her stomach and the intriguing gullies and mounds of her lower body. She left the room, a floating dream in my sleep-fogged mind. I heard her open a closet door, push clothes hangers around, and finally remove something from the closet. I floated back into sleep.

Later the smell of fresh coffee lured me to a sitting position on the side of the bed. Springs sighed with relief when I stood. I grabbed the blue jeans from the floor where they had landed the night before and pushed my way into them. In the kitchen,

I savored coffee and sought room to stretch my legs. Our knees touched as we sat at the fold-down table.

"You could wear something today besides those raggedy-ass jeans. After all, it's Sunday. Somebody I know might see me with you."

I flicked an imaginary crumb off my left knee.

"I've only worn these a couple, maybe three days," I said.

"Look, Nick, if you're going to weasel out of the band concert..."

I sat up straighter and said, "Have I ever weaseled on a promise to you?"

Maggie looked at the ceiling, lowered her gaze, and rolled her eyes as though she was about to faint. She stood and swirled, displaying slender legs under a brown, orange, and yellow dress.

"That's pretty, the way the colors blend."

"Thank you, sir. They're Fall colors."

After I finished my coffee and dressed -- in brown slacks, a beige short-sleeved shirt, and my only sports coat, we walked out into a bright new day of blue skies and drifting snow-white clouds.

"You dress up good," she said.

Heads turned as we strolled hand-in-hand toward the Methodist Church three blocks away. They weren't looking at me.

"Such a nice morning," Maggie said.

A breeze tugged gently at her shining auburn hair. She joined churchgoers on the sidewalk in front of the church, and I moseyed on to Kellogg's Drug Store. I bought a copy of the Sunday Chicago Times and strolled back to the apartment.

In the living room, I sat on the couch across from my 16-inch television. The smell of ink tweaked my nose when I opened the paper. I put the rest of it aside and turned to the sports section. The top story featured the dim prospects of the Chicago Bears having a winning season. The major league baseball season was nearly over, and the Cubs were dead again. It saddened me. I was stuck with being a fan of both teams, but should their losing make me miserable? Of course not. But it did. Guess it was a reflection on me. Made me a loser too.

Our cat, an unnamed stray with an attitude, came into the living room from some secret place, jumped onto the couch with feline ease, and placed itself against my thigh. I had read most of the paper when it jumped down, went to the door, and rubbed against Maggie's ankle when she entered. She kicked off her shoes, slipped out of her panties, pulled the dress over her head, and went into the bedroom.

"Shame," I said. "You having just come from church and all."

"I'm sorry if I embarrassed you." The words drifted back to me as she entered the bedroom to change.

Before the band concert that evening, we drove to Veteran's Cemetery on winding Harmon Road through low rolling hills south of town. Leaves hinted at the spectacular colors to come. The cemetery spread before us on the left.

"Oh, this place is beautiful. I'd forgotten. Haven't been out this way for years," Maggie cooed.

"And look at that," she added. "Those flowers are beautiful. The contrast between the silver and red. Somebody is taking loving care of that grave site."

We passed under the arch that marked the entrance. I drove around the cemetery on a one-way road before parking below the flowers she had admired.

As she removed herself from the car, she said, "I'm dying to know what we're doing here. It smells so fresh. Someone must have just mowed."

I walked up the slight incline and knelt beside the flower bed. I pulled a few weeds that weren't there the week before and reached behind the grave marker for my hand hoe. I tilled the ground around the red petunias and the silver and green dusty millers.

Maggie bent, scooped up some black dirt, and held it to her nose.

She leaned toward the grave marker and said, "Who is Caroline Miller?"

I continued to hoe and said, "All of her relatives are either dead or have moved away. She never had any children."

Maggie said, "Did you plant these flowers? Make this lovely arrangement?"

I nodded.

She rubbed her hands together to remove the last bit of soil and said, "I would never have imagined you taking care of flowers. Who is Caroline Miller? Judging from the dates on her tombstone, she'd be seventy-five if she were alive."

I pulled the last weed from the bed, tilled the soil where the weed had been, and struggled to my feet. I put the hoe back and said, "Okay, let's go to the band concert."

She rose gracefully, put her hands on her hips, glared at me, and said, "I'm not leaving until you explain. Who is Caroline Miller? Why do you take such loving care of these flowers? You won't even water my flower pots at the apartment."

"We better get going, or we'll miss the band concert," I said.

Maggie slapped her hip and said, "And, of course, you wouldn't want to do that."

"Don't be sarcastic, my dear. I promised -- so you say -- to take you to the concert, and now I'm doing it. Let's go."

I negotiated the slope toward my faithful Escort. She trotted beside me and said, "Who is Caroline Miller?"

I started the car and drove back the way we'd come. After a few blocks, we turned on Oak Glen Drive and entered the half-empty blacktop parking lot above a natural amphitheater in Oak Glen Park. Oak and elm trees rimmed the top of the west and north banks. A small lake is hemmed in on the east side. The bandstand is nestled on a stage at the back of the hollow. Twenty years old, it was kept freshly painted. The park was one of Central City's "Points of Pride."

"What about Caroline Miller? You claimed on the way here that you couldn't talk and drive at the same time. No more excuses. Tell me."

Her heels clicked as she followed me down a wide cement path, past semicircular rows of weathered wooden park benches.

"Can't talk now," I said. "Too much noise."

She scurried around me and led us to the front row. Prominent speakers stood guard at either end of a raised stage. A path led from the benches up to a concession stand. Behind the benches, a grassy slope provided space for blankets and lawn chairs.

I slouched on the bench and hoped time wouldn't stand still as we waited for the concert to begin. A breeze rustled through the trees high above and occasionally favored us with a cool kiss. Clouds, highlighted by slanting sun rays, drifted by now and then. Maggie glared at me, her eyes demanding I talk. A woman dressed in tight slacks and a striped blouse sat down. Maggie greeted her warmly. She turned and said," Nick, this is Nina Fouch. Nina, Nick Bancroft."

Nina and I exchanged greetings as she examined me. I felt like answering the question in her eyes by saying, "Maggie and me are kissing cousins." That would have been a little joke. We're not really cousins.

They chatted about how Nina loved the books Maggie chose for her daughter. The daughter, perhaps six years old, with straight brown hair and large brown eyes, squirmed her way onto my lap. She smelled of Ivory soap.

"Do you like me?" she said. Her eyes held mine until I said, "Sure."

She bounced a couple of times and said, "Bet you don't know my name."

Before I could admit my ignorance, she said, "When will the music start?"

I shrugged.

She said, "Why don't you talk to me?"

And so it went. The questions came faster than I could answer. Eventually, I just said, "Because." She countered with, "Why?"

What seemed like an hour later, but was probably only a few minutes, Nina and her daughter left to join a woman and two children several rows away. I sighed and squirmed. To kill time, I observed a variety of humans flowing down the ramp. Musical instrument cases, large and small, were attached to some. Those people dressed in black slacks -- white shirts for men, white blouses for women -- meandered behind the bandstand and eventually appeared on stage.

Sounds, at first isolated, became a raucous chorus of discordant notes and challenged the boom of a kettle drum.

I squirmed and said, "They aren't very good, are they?"

Maggie faced me, gently pushed an extended finger into my stomach, and said, "You know, smart ass, they're just tuning up. Sit up before you slide off the bench. And tell me about Caroline Miller."

"Speaking of ass, you've got a built-in cushion to sit on. I'm all muscle."

As Maggie stood, she reminded me of a slim teenager. Well, almost. A brown belt surrounded the top of her tan shorts. A black, silky blouse fitted nicely over her breasts. Tan sandals housing red toenails completed the outfit. Her hair was cropped. Women probably have a fancy name for it, but her hair was cropped to me.

I stood to keep the disfigurement of my rear from becoming permanent. A steady stream of squealing children flowed back and forth in front of and behind us. I sat and continued to squirm, trying to find a comfort zone.

Maggie said, "See, I told you we'd have to get here early for a good seat. The benches are nearly filled already."

More people filed down from the parking area and onto the benches or carried their lawn chairs and blankets to open spots on the slope.

"Yeah," I said. "Those latecomers will be sorry. They won't be able to hear a thing."

The kettle drum guy, not much taller than the drum, thumped it with a drumstick, adjusted the tightness of the skin with turnbuckle-like things, and thumped it again. The band director appeared in a matching coat and pants and a generous portion of shoulder decorations. He faced the band. A single drawn-out note sounded from one of the instruments. The others duplicated the sound. The noise from the stage ceased, and the murmur of conversation behind us dwindled. The conductor raised his baton. At last, the concert was underway. Eons later, the band members stopped making noise and talked to each other. Was it finally over? No. Just intermission.

The crowd's noise and the ruckus created by the ever-moving children returned.

"Now, mister, you will tell me who Caroline Miller was."

I sighed and knew taking her to the cemetery was a mistake. She probably wouldn't understand.

"Well," I said, "When I was a little boy, about nine or ten, I was a cute kid."

"Yeah, I'll bet. Does that have anything to do with Caroline Miller?"

"She was the one who said I was cute. She said it when I knocked on her door and asked if she wanted me to mow her grass. She lived in a bungalow on Bigelow Street."

"Nick, the intermission will be over soon. I'm not going to stop bugging you until you tell me."

I thought of that morning long ago when Mrs. Miller smiled down at me and said, "How are you going to mow my grass? You don't seem to have a mower."

I told her I thought maybe I could use hers.

"She didn't hire me to mow her grass, although I did it later. She hired me to weed her flower beds along the front and side of her house. The same flowers you saw at the cemetery."

Maggie reached across, placed her hand on mine, and said, "When she died, you started caring for her burial plot?"

"Not right away. I was in college when Mrs. Miller died. And then, I worked in Chicago. When I came back, I thought I'd look her up. When I learned she'd died, I went to the cemetery."

"And in honor of her, in memory of her, you started planting and taking care of her favorite flowers. How sweet."

"Yeah, how sweet," I said. "Now, let's settle back and listen to the concert."

She smiled.

That night she didn't stay on her side of the bed. I figured it out the next morning after she'd gone to the library. It was the band concert. Damn, and there wouldn't be another one until next summer.

MY FAVORITE SPEECH
By BOB LITER

I attended my ten-year Central City High School class reunion even though Audrey Sinclair, the chairman, scheduled the dinner at Monica's Restaurant, Central City's most refined and the scene of my worst humiliation.

Audrey had been homecoming queen, a cheerleader, and an "A" student. Her father owned Sinclair Classic Furniture, her mother was Women's Club president, and her little brother was an unrestrained champion spitball thrower.

During high school and junior college, I survived by waiting on people at the restaurant. When Audrey and her family ate there, they landed at one of my tables too often.

I heard her tell her father once after I'd run my legs off trying to do a good job, "Don't tip her too much. She'll just give the money to her drunken father."

She was wrong about that. I saved nearly all of my earnings toward college, but it was a scholarship that got me through. During our high school sophomore year, she stuck her nose up at my attempts to be friendly during study hall or lunch. No daughter of the poor was good enough for her or her group. Her boyfriend, tall, dark-haired Rob Vanders, the muscled football star, went on to State College on a football scholarship. When he graduated, they were married. I'd heard they were divorced.

As I entered the restaurant, memories of my waitress days

flooded back. Since then, I have interviewed the governor, covered major news stories in the state and nation, and received several journalism awards. I was speechless when Audrey marched up and said, "I've seated you at the speakers' table. You don't mind giving a little talk, do you?"

She smiled.

I thought of a "little talk" right then but didn't give it. I turned away and walked to the speaker's table without commenting. After all, I had no reason to be nervous. I was J.B. Bancroft, a famous girl reporter.

At the speaker's table, I sat next to an empty chair. The nameplate there said, "Dr. Jon T. Milton." Was there a Jon Milton in our class?

The choice was chicken or steak. I chose steak and ate it with delight. That's one thing I could say about the restaurant. The food was always good. Audrey nodded at me when she sat down. She nibbled at her chicken, and I was pleased to see she had gained at least ten pounds since we graduated.

Eventually, she tapped a water glass with a spoon, got the 'divided' attention of the class, and thanked all who had been 'privileged' to serve under her on the class reunion committee.

While she talked of how hard she worked on arranging the reunion, a tall man in a dark, silk suit strode past the tables, nodding at many of the occupants, and landed like a kid late for supper on the seat next to me.

"Sorry I'm late," he said, speaking to Audrey.

She gave him a sickeningly sweet smile and said, "Oh, that's all right, Jon. We all know how busy you are."

A waitress put a large steak, baked potato, and a salad in front of him.

"Excuse me," he said, talking directly to me, "I haven't had a chance to eat since breakfast. Come to think of it, I may not have had breakfast. Anyway, I'm starved."

He chewed with enthusiasm, downed a cup of coffee, got a refill, and made the ample servings on his plate disappear.

I stared straight ahead, wondering why I had come. If Audrey was envious of my career, tailored business suit, or still slim figure, she hid it well. She didn't even comment on my hairdo that cost more than I used to make in tips in a week.

Oh well, I'd sat through many a boring dinner during my reporting career. Why not one more?

The man beside me wiped his mouth with a napkin, leaned back, pushed a hand through his dark, wavy hair, looked at me, and said, "Hello."

"Doctor Jon Milton, I presume," I said.

He smiled, settled deep blue eyes on me, and said, "And you're J.B. Bancroft, the Chicago reporter. Shame we didn't get to know each other in high school."

Audrey, still standing and still talking, looked down on us and frowned. Doctor Milton leaned toward me and whispered, "She used to look down on me when we were in school. Here she is doing it again."

"And now," Audrey said, "J.B. Bancroft -- you all remember her, I'm sure -- is going to speak."

She gazed down at me like a cat above a mouse. I put my napkin aside, stood, placed the microphone at the proper angle, and said, "I doubt many of you remember me from school. I'm a reporter now for the Chicago Times."

I looked out at the audience. They didn't look any different than other audiences I'd faced. I sighed and launched into a talk about my career as a reporter.

When I finished, a smattering of applause waved across the audience. Then, after Doctor Milton stood and applauded vigorously, the applause increased. My heart was in my throat when I sat. Gone was all pretending that I didn't care.

"You've given that talk before, I'm sure," he said. "I hope I do as well."

People raised their hands.

"We don't have time for questions now. We have another speaker. Our own Doctor Milton," Audrey said.

He stood and said, "I don't have anything interesting to say. Ask your questions of Miss Bancroft. I've got some of my own."

Audrey thumped down on her chair and pouted. I had heard most of the questions before, so answering them presented no difficulty.

***

It was nearly noon the next day when I entered Doctor Milton's waiting room. I was the only one there until Audrey came from a hallway, followed by the doctor. She spotted me and said, "I thought you'd be back in Chicago by now."

Doctor Milton said, "You take those pills now, and I'm sure you'll feel better."

"Are you sick, too?" Audrey asked me.

"No, I feel fine," I said.

"She may be tired from my bending her ear last night," Doctor Milton said, "but I'm glad she's not sick. I'm taking her to lunch. And dinner, too, I hope."

WHAT WAS HE THINKING?
By **MARTIE LITER OGBORN**

Late last month, on an unusually warm day in February, even for Florida, I was on the phone with our daughter Missy. We had a long discussion concerning Gigi's advancing stages of Alzheimer's. Gigi is my husband Tom's mother. When Missy and I talk, our conversations become jewels in time, marking how gracefully Missy is growing into a delightful and compassionate woman. She and I are both petite, although her long blond hair is curlier, and we have the same "cat swallowed the canary" smile.

I remember, like yesterday, a conversation about Gigi. Missy had turned six the day after Easter when she said, "Mommy, Gigi is so smart. Every time she comes to visit, she wants me to get a book from the bookshelf. When I sit close, she opens the book and reads the whole thing. She never misses any words. Remember yesterday, Mommy, she carried my Easter basket for me. We found lots of pretty eggs in our yard. She knows really good places to look, like behind the flagpole in the yellow flowers. I love Gigi!"

Now, 30 years later, we share the same joy in our voices, but it is softened with concern when we speak of Tom's mother. Gigi is much more apprehensive and, at times, overly cautious about what she says and what she does. At 87, you can see it in her eyes, a faded, dull stare, as if she is looking for answers. But answers to what?

After my conversation with Missy, the rest of the day was followed by a yearly activity, almost a ritual. Neighbors in our mobile home community gather at the boat slip to prepare pontoons for the new season. Tom and I enjoyed our pontoon boat; it was time to prepare it for the inaugural launch of the new year.

Tom took the charged batteries to the boat slip several blocks from our house, the first of many trips with our golf cart. As the weeks passed, Tom and the golf cart were gone more every day.

Even though last year Tom and I had carefully covered and stored the boat, every year, there is a long list of chores to do. Tom usually left in the morning. When he wasn't cleaning and removing debris from the boat floor, he was wiping down surfaces or checking little nooks for pests. For a week, Tom returned late in the afternoon with a beer and a story to share about the latest scuttlebutt in the park.

Last night after dinner, sitting on the front porch with a Miller Lite, I said, "I think we need a second golf cart." Like Tom does at times, he cocked his head, his smile lit up surrounded by his white goatee and mustache, but this time in his eyes, you could see a faded, dull stare. There was a brief pause in the conversation. The subject changed to the clubhouse being closed until further notice and something about social distancing.

The next day, Friday, March 13th, Tom slipped next door while I cleaned up after breakfast. He was talking to our neighbor and mentioned to Jimmy he needed one of his golf carts. It seemed like Jimmy had a corral of golf carts.

Tom again said, "I need one of your golf carts."

Jimmy said, "Sure, help yourself. Use it as long as you need it."

Tom shook his head, "I want to buy one."

"Oh, okay. Which one?"

"How about the blue one?" Tom said. They shook hands, and Tom drove the golf cart home. He parked it under our screened-in carport.

When he came into the house, he tossed me a strange set of

keys. There was a different look in his eyes. I recognized the familiar twinkle; he took the toothpick out of his mouth and said, "I bought you a golf cart. It's blue!"

"What were you thinking?" I said.

With the toothpick back in his mouth, he laughed and said, "Sandy, you thought I wasn't listening to last night. I wasn't about to tell you that you were right. So, I decided I would surprise you."

"I'm not sure what has surprised me more, you telling me I was right or you buying a second golf cart."

That afternoon I talked to Missy. She could tell there was edginess in my voice when I said, "I don't know what your Dad was thinking!"

I had hardly gotten the words out when I heard a gasp on the other end of the phone. Then dead silence. I quickly remembered our last conversation about Gigi, Alzheimer's, and the tendency for it to be hereditary.

Missy began spouting questions, "Is Dad okay? Is he upset? Are you upset?" When she took a breath, I interjected, "Everything is fine."

"Let me tell you what your "crazy dad" did today. Last night I didn't think he was listening when I said we needed two golf carts. Today he bought a second golf cart from the neighbor. And you know how your dad is; he gets the biggest kick out of surprising me."

It was easy to reassure her everything was okay. We both laughed like tuned wind chimes. Then, at the same time, we said, "WHAT WAS HE THINKING?"

THANKSGIVING WITH THE BANCROFT'S
By **MARTIE LITER OGBORN**

My name is J.B. Bancroft. J.B. stands for Jillian Bernice; I hate the name Bernice, so I have chosen to go by J.B. You might be familiar with my Uncle Nick Bancroft. He is an investigative reporter in Central City, IL.

A few years ago, when I entered ICC as a freshman, Uncle Nick inherited a detective agency, AAA Investigations. Family dinners have never been the same. Get-togethers at Thanksgiving are much more exciting. We gathered around the table this year and heatedly discussed Nick's latest case. He called it "Death Sting."

In the past, just like many families, during the holidays, we would travel to a convenient location or the location of a patriarch or matriarch of the family. My dad, Joe Bancroft (Uncle Nick's brother), and mom, Donna Bancroft, would take us three kids, Jeff, me - J.B., and my little sister Jeannie to Des Moines, Iowa.

Bernice Bancroft, whom we called Grandma "B," decreed that the entire family drive to her house each Thanksgiving for dinner. The food was always so scrumptious. After several hours, we would finally arrive and get out of the car. Our family would go from the frigid, barren outside into the overheated wonderland of Grandma's house, carrying packages and Mom's crescent rolls. When I went in the back door and up the three steps to the kitchen, the wonderful smells would almost knock me over.

For most of my life, when I would see Grandma, the first words I would hear were, "Well, Jillian Bernice, don't just stand in the middle of the doorway! Go to the side room where the kid's table is set up." That would be where my brother Jeff, four years older, and my sister Jeannie, two years younger, were also curtly directed and, without ceremony, dismissed.

Our second cousins arrived earlier and would have already found their places at the miniature table. I think they belonged to someone Dad calls Cousin George. Kenny, Cheryl, and Little George were about our same age. We would take off our coats and pile them up in the corner until Grandma "B" would come in and not nicely remind us to use the coat closet.

My brother, sister and I had been cooped up in the car for hours, and we were already on each other's last nerve. Dad, always impatient to get the drive to Des Moines over, wouldn't make any stops. It was not easy for my sister and me to pee in a coffee can. And because Jeannie was embarrassed, we brought an extra towel so I could hold it up as a curtain for her. Jeff would snicker.

Now asking us to sit so soon after getting out of the car was asking a lot. I would trudge to a seat at the very short table, shaking my head. I would be thinking of other silly stuff that took place during the car ride. To this day, I will never understand why my sister insisted on sleeping on the backseat floor. Jeannie couldn't stretch out, so she would claim the floorboard and lay her stomach over the hump. Jeff and I would have to make sure we didn't step on her. I can't remember where we put our feet!

The six cousins sitting at the kid's table would be fidgeting. We would never really have anything to talk about, but still, we would try to remember each other's names. This was way before electronic devices; staring was a game. We wanted to check each other out and not get caught. Looking back, I may have had a crush on Kenny. I might have even blushed when I caught him looking at me.

What I do remember, for sure, is that Thanksgiving dinner was worth the wait. When our parents brought in our prepared plates, heaped with warm delicacies, they would light the little candles on the table. The candles were shaped like a little pilgrim boy and girl. After grace was said, somehow, six little Indians turned into happy, grateful, almost well-behaved young folks. Jeannie would ask why the butter tasted so different, and every year Mom would explain Grandma "B" has REAL butter. We would enjoy the cranberry orange Jell-O, smile, and watch the pilgrim hats of the candles melt.

Bancroft Thanksgiving traditions have melted into twenty years of fond memories with a promise of many more.

WHERE ARE THEY NOW?
By **MARTIE LITER OGBORN**

Our conversation was as delicious as the juicy steaks we ordered during dinner last night at Monica's. Before our hostess served the salad, we had written a list of classmates' names and started playing "Where Are They Now?" Natasha and Jon provided details: who they married, how many kids they had, and where they lived.

I wasn't much help. I had been away from Central City for over 5 years. My name is J.B. Bancroft. I just returned home to claim my inheritance, AAA Investigations, a one-man detective agency. Natasha, my friend since fifth grade, and Jon, a guy I dated during our senior year of high school, volunteered on my welcoming committee and took me to dinner. Over the main course, we shared comical stories and reminisced about follies and friends from our graduating class of 1995.

Before coffee and dessert arrived, Natasha leaned in to ask about Stephen Branlin. "In the study hall, you were always writing letters to Steve. He was ahead of us by a couple of years." And when she said, "He was a marine, right?" her smile broadened, and her eyebrows went up and down. My face turned almost as red as the nail polish I was wearing. My carefully selected outfit was a red sweater and black slacks, a meager attempt at school pride. Central City High School's colors are red and black.

Jon gave me a suspicious look and a frown, but as soon as I said, "Jon, you remember Steve? I was writing to him two years before we started dating. He went into the service in 1992." Jon's eyes sparkled again, and he sat back comfortably in his chair, sipping his coffee. Natasha pulled her chair in closer, with her elbows on the table; she put her chin in her hands.

"All right," I said, "I haven't thought about Steve for a while. He was such a class clown, but he was smart in many subjects, just not Geometry. In my Freshman year, he was a Senior in my Unified Geometry class. The final semester we studied together, and we both finished with a grade of 95%."

Jon smiled again, picked up a cylinder-shaped white salt shaker, and asked, "What's the formula for the volume."

"You know as well as I do, $V=Bh$, you finished Unified Geometry with 104%! Couldn't resist those extra credit problems, could you?" He said, "Go on."

"When Steve left for basic training after graduation, he asked everyone to write. I started writing and kept on writing. He told some funny stories when he wrote back. He wasn't allowed to smile except in church, and one time, because his DI told him to, he just about knocked somebody's block off with a pugil stick in hand-to-hand practice."

"In one letter, he gave me explicit directions on how to send him cookies for his birthday, August 3rd. I wasn't supposed to mention it was his birthday. That was very important, and I had to write the letter exactly like this: Steve, I know I am NOT SUPPOSED TO SEND FOOD, but I thought it was worth a try. There are at least 12 dozen cookies. There should be enough for everyone in the platoon, and I packed a box with a dozen cookies for the SDI and the DI."

I heard from him a few more times before he graduated from basic training on August 19th. I remember the date because we continue to write for another year. The last letter I received from him was dated August 19, 1993.

I picked up my fork to taste the cherry cheesecake we shared, and Natasha picked up the conversation. "I remember when

Steve came back from basic training late summer of 1992. Marsha Townsend and Steve had a beautiful wedding before he returned to Camp Pendleton. You and Marsha got to be good friends."

"Yes, we stayed in touch after the wedding, and I continued to write to Steve through my sophomore year. On October 4, 1993, I was with Marsha when she got the news."

The day before, Steve was with special operation forces, Humvees, and trucks under Lieutenant Colonel McKnight's command. The U.S. Marine Corps had secured nearly one-third of Mogadishu to facilitate airlifted humanitarian supplies for starving Somalis. Standing in the way was a military faction that refused to cooperate with the UN. On October 3, 1993, the special ops members arrived at the targeted location to take an assault team and their prisoners back to base. The entire mission was to take no longer than 30 minutes, but it lasted into the night. The next day U.S. forces were finally evacuated to the U.N. base by an armored convoy. Nineteen U.S. soldiers were killed during the battle or shortly after, and another 73 were wounded in action.

The wait for word about Steve on October 4, 1993, was terrible. Would we honor him on Memorial Day or Veteran's Day? Marsha's husband, Master Sergeant Stephen Branlin, still serves in the Marines. Marsha and Steve live happily in California with their 2 boys and a little girl.

MURDER BY THE BOOK - CHAPTER ONE

A Nick Bancroft Mystery

By **BOB LITER**

Tires screeched as I started across Commerce Street on my way to Otto's Tavern for breakfast. I jumped back to the curb. Half a block to my left, a battered pickup truck swerved around a man running in the middle of the street. Damn. It was Broadway John. His canvas shoes slapped the hot, cracked pavement with each uneven stride. The truck, loaded with junk for the scrap yard, rattled by.

Broadway John pulled up, gasping for air.

"Mr., I think she's dead. She lost her clothes, and she's like a stiff dog I found once," he said.

"What do you mean, 'she's dead?' Who?"

"She's all stiff and cold, like the dog."

"Who?"

"I don't know."

"All right, just calm down."

"She's at the football stadium, sitting in the first row. Doubled up with a book in her lap. You know, Central City High, up on the bluff. I was looking for cans."

He carried his usual plastic garbage bag. It was empty. I ignored the lack of logic in looking for aluminum cans, in

August, at a football stadium. I didn't want to get involved, damn it. I didn't want to hurt his feelings either.

"Come on," I said. "We'll drive up there."

I retrieved my ancient Escort from behind the nearly abandoned office building I had just left. The car sputtered the ten blocks or so to the stadium. We parked at the gate beside a police patrol car. Broadway John, or BJ as I called him, was trying to force a pair of thick eyeglasses onto his face.

"Look what I found," he said proudly, holding them toward me.

"Don't try to wear them. They're too small. They'll give you a headache. Come on."

The football field was surrounded by a link fence, but the gate was open. We crossed the cinder track and headed toward the wooden bleachers on the grassy field. BJ trotted ahead. A policeman standing on the cinder track stopped him. The crime-scene tape was stretched from the top of the bleachers to a stake driven into the track and then back to the top.

When I caught up, BJ insisted, "She was right there, right there." He pointed to the front row of the stands near the 50-yard line. Tears joined perspiration on his face.

"I believe you, BJ. Police must have taken the body away. Let's go back to the car."

"What does he know about this?" the cop, a young patrolman I didn't know, asked. "There was a body. Homicide has been here and left. The body was taken to the morgue."

I explained that BJ saw the body when he was looking for aluminum cans.

"I'll give Detective Andy Brown all the details, but I want to get BJ out of here, okay?" The cop took our names and reluctantly allowed us to leave.

BJ still was confused about what had happened to the body. I changed the subject.

"Don't look for cans at the football stadium in the summer. You'll find more in Hellerman Park. Don't stay around there too long, either. Remember, I told you to stay away from there when the bad guys come."

When we got to Hellerman Park, a block-square playground taken over at night by drug dealers, he was humming a tune I couldn't quite place. I left him there and returned to what I had started to do, get breakfast at the tavern. I told BJ's story to Otto Kamp, the bar owner, as I gnawed on a doughnut almost as stale as the air in the place.

"I suppose you want another cup of coffee," Otto said. I nodded. He added another figure to my tab.

"You better call Brown."

"Yeah, I guess I should."

I called Detective Andrew Brown, Central City, Illinois' finest. I explained how BJ found the body and how the police had already taken it to the morgue when I returned BJ to the scene. Brown said a woman who runs every morning there called in.

"She must have been there right after BJ. I don't suppose it will help to talk to him but bring him in just in case," Andy said.

I agreed and figured that would be the end of my involvement. Sure, and I'd also win the lottery.

The next morning I sat at Otto's bar reading the Central City Press sports pages. Otto sat in a worn, cushioned chair behind the bar. A wall lamp cast shadows beyond his ancient head. He commented from time to time on the news in the newspaper's front section. I was trying not to listen. I was perturbed because there was no report on Milwaukee Professional Bowlers' Association national tournament. The finals were to be on television the following Saturday. It pissed me off that the paper had room for local dart ball results but no room for a national bowling tournament.

It was around 10 o'clock. The sun partially penetrated the dirt on the front windows. I know because I was looking in that direction, composing in my mind the blistering letter to the newspaper I would never write. A man I later learned was Ramsey Sinclair opened the front door, hesitated, allowing sunlight to actually enter the place, and said in a voice that carried to every corner, "Is Nick Bancroft here?"

That's me. I couldn't see much against the light, but I noted the classy cut of his suit and decided it looked too expensive to be owned by a bill collector.

Still, I hesitated to answer. He said, "Well, surely the question is not that difficult for you two ... gentlemen."

"I'm Nick Bancroft," I said.

"Could I tear you away from all this and back to your office long enough to discuss business?"

I stiffened.

Otto must have noticed. He said, "Mr. Bancroft was just saying it's time for him to get back to work."

Sinclair turned and left. I followed in the wake of his long strides as we crossed the street, went up the creaking wooden stairs, past the Ballard Inc. office, on the second floor, and up to the third floor.

The notice from my office door informing potential customers I could be found at Otto's was on the floor. A dirty, chipped blue bowl near the note reminded me I forgot to feed the cat.

My office consisted of a worn, oversized wooden desk with drawers that stuck, a swivel chair that didn't always swivel, and some battered filing cabinets. In front of the desk was a wooden chair for the occasional visitor. A radio with a cracked plastic case sat on the window ledge beside an ancient air-conditioner. The window overlooked the parking lot at the back of the building. A one-room apartment adjoined the office. The rest of the third floor housed cobwebs and dust.

I settled behind the desk. After looking at the "guest" chair, Sinclair rejected my offer to sit. He was slender and a shade over six feet tall. His hair and eyebrows were black. Touches of silver highlighted his sideburns. His close-set, penetrating eyes glared at me. His thin lips were turned down, reminding me of a drama mask.

He asked me to investigate the murder of his daughter, Linsley. "I'm sure you know about it by now. Her body was found at the football stadium. I'm from Chicago, but I used to live in this town years ago and have contacts. I'm told you're the person most likely to find out who killed my daughter."

I said, "First, you should know, just for the record, that I am not a licensed private investigator. I'm an ex-reporter who inherited this sorry office from a friend I occasionally worked with. He died and had the bad taste to leave me his dying detective agency. It offered me a chance to live here for a while and quit the entertainment business that passes as news."

Sinclair didn't need to know the place was rent-free for a few more months because my benefactor had paid it in advance and that I was just drifting until the rent ran out.

He informed me he knew all the details about my squalid existence – he didn't actually say squalid, just implied it – and said he wanted an answer.

I said, "Yes."

"I'll pay you two hundred dollars a day. I expect a telephone report tomorrow at four o'clock. Four o'clock. Don't make me wait. I'll deduct from your pay for every second I wait for your call."

He handed me an envelope and left. It contained ten one-hundred dollar bills and a card bearing his name and phone number.

I stuffed the money into my billfold, took a can of cat food from the filing cabinet, opened the thing, and put the stuff in the bowl. My cat responsibilities were met for another day. I went across the street to Otto's and my favorite stool.

"Now tell me again how much I owe you, Mr. Bartender," I said.

"I suppose you want another cup of coffee."

I fanned the bills near his face.

"Here's a hundred, my man. It was twenty-six dollars for coffee and those things you call doughnuts and seventy-three for beer, right? You may not keep the change. However, get a beer on me, and I'll have one."

Otto stared at the money. "It's too early for beer for you ... or me. That guy hire you to rob a bank? Pay you in advance? Thanks for taking care of me before you pay the others."

"You and the office utilities are the ones I pay first."

He put the money in his billfold, took a dollar out of the cash register, and handed it to me. He tore up the tab that had been next to the cash register for several weeks.

He placed a cup of coffee in front of me. "On the house," he said.

"Sure, now that I have the money, you offer free coffee. When I'm broke, you charge it to my account. Great."

Otto turned to his chair behind the bar, sighed, and sat down. He was at least 60 years old, judging from his wrinkled face, although we never discussed his age. He probably weighed 200 pounds even though he was slightly more than five feet tall. He wore baggy pants, a pair of squashed shoes, and T-shirts that advertised things. For some reason, I liked the guy. Maybe he was a father image.

I told him about the case. He got up and riffled through newspapers on a small table near his chair. "Ya, here it is." He handed me the newspaper section containing the report on the death of Linsley Sinclair. The paper identified her as a 33-year-old resident of Central City. The cause of death, according to the report, was still under investigation.

Detective Andrew Brown was quoted, but, as usual, he didn't offer much. Brown and I had argued many times about his withholding information that, in my opinion, belonged to the public.

"Wow," Otto said. "You're in the big league at last. I may never have to loan you beer money again."

"Yes, but I may not be big league long. Sinclair didn't allow me to explain that I probably can't find out more than the police. Brown is on the case, and he's good."

"You solved the Anderson case when you were a reporter. Why not this one?"

"Yeah, why not," I said as I slid from the bar stool and left.

The sun did a job on my eyes before they adjusted; otherwise, I might have avoided BJ. Still, I had promised to take him to the police station. The poor guy thinks I'm the greatest thing since the last Broadway musical because I did a piece on him a couple of years ago when I still worked for a living. He's been a character around the downtown area for more years than anyone can remember. He's big, bony, has a hawk nose, but has the mind of a child – a sweet, harmless child.

He knew a bushel of Broadway songs from musicals and usually sang at least one whenever we met. His real name was John Snyder. He walked with me and sang to himself, lost in his own musical world. Apparently, he had forgotten about the body.

We walked by a pool hall, a couple of taverns as forlorn as Otto's, Lou's Restaurant, and several boarded-up businesses to get to the police station three blocks away.

The cement steps leading to the station were worn from constant traffic over the years. I climbed them once again.

"Hey, where you been?" asked the desk sergeant, a guy named Morris, as we entered the main room with its high ceiling, soiled windows, and scattered desks.

The ringing of telephones, the hum of conversation, occasional shouting, and the long counter designed to keep the public at bay reminded me that maybe I missed the place. I had spent a lot of time there as a reporter.

Morris gave me the prepared-for-the-media reports on Linsley Sinclair's murder. I leaned against the counter as I read them and wrote in a small notebook. He gave me a questioning look as BJ continued his singsong routine. When I finished, BJ and I went to Brown's office around the counter. Brown talked to him briefly.

"What a witness he would make," Brown said after BJ left when I told him we had private business. I invited Brown for a cup of coffee at the Lucky Diner across the street. It has been there forever and probably never passed a health department test, but at least it was convenient. After we got the coffee, I informed Andy that Ramsey Sinclair had hired me to find out who killed his daughter.

Andy, who is about my height and weight, five feet ten and 180 pounds, and about my age, late thirties, put his left hand on top of his bald head and said, "Why in the world would he hire a broken down bowler to investigate anything?"

"He's heard how good I am, I suppose."

"How good you are? The lawyers seem to think you're capable of investigating traffic accidents. Desperate people sometimes hire you to gather divorce evidence, but a murder?"

Andy, with his angry dark eyes and jutting chin, intimidated witnesses. He also intimidated most reporters and other low types. However, I had learned to get past his tough exterior and was no longer awed by him.

"I read all the police reports. Tell me what the reports don't say."

It annoyed me the need to beg for information from "public servants." It was no different when I questioned Andy, although he was less arrogant and self-serving than most.

"How much is this guy paying you to tell him what police have found out so far?" Andy asked.

"Enough, so I don't mind buying you coffee. Sinclair demanded that I give him a report by tomorrow afternoon. You always know more than you tell reporters. Give me a break. I'll sell this story to one of the Chicago papers if it is good enough. I can make you a hero."

"Would you do that for me? Gee, wouldn't that be swell." He leaned toward me. "The victim's mother lives here. She's in the phone book. Mrs. Ramsey Sinclair. She's divorced. Never remarried. And there is this thing you must promise to keep quiet, at least for now."

I nodded. I had almost always kept the promises I made to Andy. An overhead fan groaned as it pushed hot air our way. The skinny, redheaded waitress behind the counter laughed as she talked to a customer. I waited.

"There were no marks on the body except a small one on the left arm, like a pinprick. The lab people will probably find something lethal injected into her system. And whoever killed her put a sex etiquette book on her lap."

A sex etiquette book. No wonder Andy had kept it quiet so far. The media would have a ball with that.

"Anything you find out, you give me, right?"

I agreed. Before it was over, he held out on me, and I returned the favor.

AUGUST IS MURDER - CHAPTER ONE

A Nick Bancroft Mystery
By **BOB LITER**

The first time they tried to kill me, I was asleep. My office and apartment were on the third floor of a nearly abandoned building. My own coughing jarred me awake. I rolled to a sitting position from the sweat-wet bedding and continued choking on hot, acrid air. The sweat was no surprise. My air conditioner had quit. But this was more than August heat in Central City, Illinois.

A flip of the light switch near my bed did nothing to alleviate the darkness. I went to my hands and knees and felt around until I found my pants and shoes, sat against the bed, squirmed into the jeans, and put on my much-used Reeboks. The heat from the floor threatened to roast my rump.

"Don't panic, Nick," I said aloud. Should I try to save anything or just get the hell out? My files, I had to save my case files. The dented metal filing cabinet in the office contained stuff from the previous owner. Still, I just wanted my own files in the top drawer. I crawled into the office, stood, and pulled out the top drawer. I felt my way to the office door and opened it. A swish of even hotter air swept against my face. The drawer slipped from my hands, but I kept it from falling to the floor with my knee.

What about Maggie? She might be in the office on the second floor. It was well past midnight. Why would she be there? I assured myself she was not. She was why I now had a stray cat and a cracked heart. What about the cat? But there was no need to worry about it. Any cat that came and went when the office door was locked wouldn't be trapped in that old building.

A flickering light appeared as I neared the stairway. Hungry flames licked at the air below, daring me to try to escape in that direction. Fire noise rose like the vicious growl of a watchdog.

"Don't panic," I repeated.

My lungs felt as though they were melting. Heat pushed me back like an unseen hand. The fire escape! Where was it? On the side of the building at the end of the hall? Beyond my office and all that unoccupied space? I remembered rust, lots of rust. What a choice. Walk down the stairs into an inferno or risk falling three floors from a fire escape that probably hadn't been used in twenty years.

I felt my way to the end of the hallway. The door wouldn't budge. Could I crawl through the door window? I smashed the file drawer against the glass, shattering it. Hot air swished out of the building through the opening.

I placed the drawer on the floor and removed shards of glass until I figured there was enough room to climb out. I felt around outside, trying to locate something solid. Nothing. Light from the fire had not yet penetrated the darkness on that side of the building. Was the fire escape really there? I picked up the file drawer and dropped it outside the window, hoping it would hit the fire escape landing if it was there. The file drawer thudded against something almost immediately.

I used the doorknob to steady myself and raised one leg through the window. Muscles complained as I maneuvered the other leg through. Broken glass ripped my pants and scratched my legs and stomach as I wiggled out into the darkness.

I grasped the base of the window frame and rested my knees against the outside of the door. I lowered my feet an inch at a time. If my legs extended completely and my feet still hadn't touched anything, could I pull myself back up?

My feet made contact with something solid. The platform? I tested it with my weight as I held onto the window ledge in case the thing below me, whatever it was, gave way.

I released one hand from the ledge. It was sticky. I reached down and tried to feel whatever was supporting my feet, but I couldn't reach it unless I let go. I took a deep breath, released my grip on the window ledge, and sank to my knees on metal – crusty metal. The fire escape landing.

The filing cabinet drawer sat near the steps leading down. Holding the rail with one hand, I carried the drawer in the other arm and made my way down, one step at a time, toward a glow coming from inside the building. Flickering light cast shadows on the second-floor fire escape platform. I put the file drawer on the landing and crept onto the fire escape extension straight out into the night. Would the rust give way and allow my weight to swing the extension down to the ground? About halfway out, the damned thing dropped without warning. I squeezed the rusted metal railings until the pain in my blood-soaked hands forced a scream from my parched lips. The noise evaporated into the smoky night. The extension jolted to an abrupt halt. It was headed downward at an angle that left me about 20 feet above the ground.

I climbed back up, retrieved the file drawer, and climbed down cautiously, one step at a time, fearing the ladder would drop violently at any moment. When I was almost to the end, it descended at a slow, comfortable pace and stopped about two feet from the ground. I stepped onto the blessed gravel and expected the ladder to spring back up. It didn't. Firelight made it easy to make my way to the front of the building. I ran awkwardly away from the heat and flames.

The hungry blaze ate at the building and its contents. My stuff was in there. My clothes, a couple of bowling balls I no longer bothered to keep in the rear of my car, a radio, an old wooden chair, my bed, and a refrigerator. And the desk. My good old desk. The fire would consume them all.

DEATH STING - CHAPTER ONE
A Nick Bancroft Mystery
By **BOB LITER**

"However, according to the coroner, it wasn't the bee stings that killed her. She apparently died from a heart attack brought on by stress."

Maggie Atley, who sat across from me at the fold-down kitchen table in my apartment, lowered the latest copy of Better Homes and Gardens.

"What?"

"The body was found in a field southwest of town, according to the Central City Press. In other words, this woman was scared to death."

"What a horrible way to die," Maggie said. "Who was she?"

She marked her place in the magazine with one of my latest past due bills, put the magazine down, lifted her coffee cup, and sipped. She frowned, said, "Yuk," got up, went to the counter, poured the coffee from her cup into the coffee maker, refilled her cup, and returned.

"Her name, if you must know, was Vicki Fowler. Twenty-three years old from Springfield. She lived here at the Good Shepherd Home."

"Springfield, Illinois?"

"Yes. Don't you find it intriguing that a woman was found dead practically outside our door with bee stings all over her body?"

Maggie pushed light brown hair from her forehead and sighed. "Intriguing, yes, and I know what you're thinking," she said.

"You always think you know what I'm thinking."

She put her elbows on the table, held the cup in both hands, and smiled that knowing smile I loved.

"You're thinking there's a story in this you can sell to the Chicago Times. You're planning right now to start an investigation into this bee-sting thing and neglect the work that brings in steady money, work that pays the bills. Right, Nick? It's your business, of course, but you need money."

When we first met, I thought I would like to get in her pants – to coin a phrase – and her heavenly blue eyes, sparkling with amusement, told me she read my thoughts. Instead of pretending to be offended, she smiled.

Now I admired her freshly scrubbed face. She was a knockout when her hair was teased into a semblance of obedience, and she wore that eye shadow stuff and the rest of it. But at breakfast, with tousled hair and freckles on her cheeks, unhidden by makeup, she was *woman*.

She was right about my plans to pursue the story. "Well, why not?" I said. "There surely is more to the story than what they've printed here."

As it turned out, there was a hell of a lot more. If I'd known the players and their eventual desire to kill me, well, I would have thought about it.

Maggie was my part-time secretary, lover, and would-be slave driver. She lived with me at the moment but insisted it was not a permanent arrangement, which was fine with me, I thought.

My name is Nick Bancroft. I'm an ex-reporter who inherited a run-down one-man detective agency in Central City, Illinois. I am a couple of years older than Maggie's "nearly forty."

"What about those pictures you promised that attorney?" Maggie asked, "the ones of the broken sidewalk. And you have two traffic-accident photo jobs."

I finished my coffee and squeezed out from under the table. I kissed her forehead on my way to the office in the front of the apartment, taking the newspaper with me.

    She was right. I had to get to work, and I would in a minute or two, but first, I had to consider the possibilities of the bee-sting story. How would a woman get bee stings all over her body and wind up dead in a nearby farm field? Where did the bees come from?

    My nameless cat jumped onto the desk, sat, and waited. I petted it automatically. The cat had trained me well. It was an independent thing, primarily white with a black ear and an attitude. Maggie had foisted it on me back at my old office. It wouldn't let me touch it for weeks even though it showed up regularly to be fed. I refused to name the ungrateful beggar, much to Maggie's annoyance. She called it Ruffles until I convinced her it was male.

    Maggie appeared in the office doorway, leaned against the jamb, and sighed. "You pay more attention to that cat than to me. When you head out to slay dragons, I want more than a peck on the forehead."

    She glided into the room, petted the cat, and sat on my lap. Her one-hundred-and-twenty or so pounds settled in as we kissed. I tasted coffee and smelled Dial soap, the soap we had used to shower together before breakfast. I enjoyed washing away the sweat her body created when she ran her usual two miles before I got out of bed.

    We sat, as we often had since she came to live with me, and watched through the large front window as a variety of shoes and ankles marched past on the sidewalk above. The stairs from the walk led down, and by the window and its black block lettering advertising my business: "AAA Investigations."

    My office consisted of an old wooden desk, a couple of file cabinets, an outdated Dell computer, a Canon printer, and a Motorola radio in a cracked plastic case.

    "Okay, boss, I'll get the mundane stuff done and then see what I can find out about how and why a woman winds up scared to death by bees."

    Maggie placed her warm, moist lips on mine. I caressed a well-formed breast before she pulled away, stood, and said, "Oh no, you don't. We've both got other things to do."

She placed one hand atop her head and sashayed out of the room. I downed the rest of the coffee and left the cup on my desk. She'd see it later, take it to the kitchen, and insist she wasn't going to chase all over the apartment picking up dirty cups I left behind. Life was good ... then.

A POINT OF MURDER - CHAPTER ONE

A Nick Bancroft Mystery
By **BOB LITER**

The day I can't forget began with a slap on my bare ass that stung me awake. Maggie Atley, dressed in a smile, jumped back from the bed, leaned her face toward mine, and said, "Get up, you lazy bum. Have some coffee ready when I get back."

I turned away, buried my head in her pillow, and assumed a fetal position. I made snoring noises and breathed in the fragrance of her apple-scented shampoo.

"Please," she cooed.

I moved to the edge of the bed, sat up, and rubbed my eyes. She backed away and fought for balance as she hopped into a pair of faded red sweatpants. She pulled a matching sweatshirt over her short, auburn hair, shoulders, breasts, and stomach. I faked a lunge. She grabbed running shoes from a chair and dodged away. She leaned against the door jamb as she put them on. Musical laughter faded as I heard her prance through the basement apartment, the office, out the front door, and up the steps for her morning run.

In the kitchen, as the coffee perked, a cumulus cloud cruised past the window in the vastness of a blue sky. It was a welcome change from the May rains that had drenched Central City and much of Illinois for four days.

I nursed a cup of coffee and anticipated the feel of Maggie's flesh when she returned. I'd peel off her sweat-wet clothes and...

The phone rang. I lifted the receiver reluctantly and heard Central City's one-man detective bureau, Andy Brown, say, "Got a body I want you to see before we move it."

"Where?"

"In the alley behind that tavern where you used to hang out."

"Right. I'm on my way."

I jumped into blue jeans, grabbed a fresh T-shirt, shoved my feet into a pair of worn Reeboks, and ran out of the office to the back of the building and my ancient red Escort.

He wanted me at a crime scene. A body, he said. Probably some poor bum whose liver gave out. Hardly a major story. The Chicago Times, the newspaper that bought most of my freelance stuff, probably wouldn't print it. Still, I had to make the scene to satisfy Brown, my main police source.

I drove south on University Street and saw only one other moving vehicle, a white Nelson Dairy truck. It stopped, and a young guy jumped out. He raced across the street in front of me, a bottle of milk in each hand. He waved after I slammed on the brakes. Three blocks later, I turned left on Incline Drive. From there, it was downhill for four blocks to Commerce Street. My car only stalled at one stop light.

My name is Nick Bancroft. Before meeting Maggie, I had belittled myself for returning to Central City to escape the horror of reporting everyday crimes in Chicago. Now, back in my hometown, I pecked out a pressure-free living selling pieces to the Times and operating a half-ass one-man detective agency.

A young cop I didn't know stepped in front of my car and held up a hand as I eased into the alley behind Commerce Street. "Sorry, sir, you can't use this alley now."

"Captain Brown called me. Where can I park?"

"You Nick Bancroft?"

I admitted it.

"He said you'd be coming."

He hesitated, pointed to a space off the alley between two abandoned buildings, and said, "There, I guess. You'll have to walk the rest of the way."

I parked, hoping nothing in the debris would puncture my tires, wormed my way out of the car, and trotted toward the other end of the block where several uniforms had gathered. One was writing in a notebook, and Brown, with his arms folded across his chest, was talking to Coroner John Connor. An ambulance was parked off to the side. Paramedics stood by.

A uniformed arm blocked my path. I told the cop – I couldn't remember his name – "Brown sent for me."

"Over there." He pointed.

Yellow crime-scene tape blocked the way. Somehow, always in Chicago and usually here in Central City, whoever strung the damned stuff managed to get it high enough to make it difficult to step over but low enough to make it awkward to duck under. I managed to scissor over it.

"Ever see anything like this in Chicago?" Brown said as I approached.

His cigar, level with my chin, emitted foul smoke. I stepped back. He pointed at a pair of worn running shoes attached to the body of a teenage boy sprawled on his back in the dirt to the side of the alley. The heels touched, the toes angled out. My gaze jumped past blue jeans to where the boy's arms sprawled from a soiled St. Louis Cardinals T-shirt, the hands clenched. The light brown face was tilted to one side. A galvanized spike extended from the left temple. Two flies nibbled on a bit of dried blood near the point where the spike violated the head.

Brown steadied me and said, "Sorry. Didn't know this would shake you that much."

I knelt, tilted my head, and stared into Bobby Scalf's unseeing eyes. Tears formed in mine. I wanted to hold his head and rub the tight curls as I had only a few days before, but I couldn't disturb the scene.

"Have you identified the victim?" I repeated the question before Brown said, "Not yet. I wanted you to see this because, as you know, the Central City Press will play it down. Trudi Seymour wouldn't want to soil the image of *her* city."

I stood, wiped my eyes, and said, "I know this kid. He's Bobby Scalf. Was Bobby Scalf."

"Are you sure? I figured we'd spend half the day trying to ID him. How come you know him? You familiar with the gang murders in Chicago that involve spikes?"

"I've never been at the scene of one before, but I've heard of them."

"I'll want a statement detailing how you knew him. You're pale as a sheet. Come to the station in about an hour. I'll get your statement then."

I nodded. My eyes were drawn again to the spike protruding from the temple of the kid who wanted to be like me.

AND THE BAND PLAYED ON - CHAPTER ONE

A Nick Bancroft Mystery
By **BOB LITER**

I witnessed the murder of Irene Donovan because I'd made a promise to "sometime" take Maggie Atley to a band concert. Maggie, a librarian, divorcee, and my talented lover insisted I take her, "Because the outdoor band concert season is almost over."

She wiped an imaginary tear from under her right eye and said, "Please, Nick."

You'd think I'd be smart enough to withhold promises I didn't intend to keep.

* * *

I'm Nick Bancroft. In my hometown, Central City, Illinois, I squeezed out a leisurely living as a freelance reporter and private investigator.

"You lack ambition," Maggie sometimes reminds me, "but I don't care because my ex-husband was overwhelmed by it and never had time for me."

"Did I really promise to take you to a band concert?" I said as I sipped coffee and sought room to stretch my legs during a leisurely Sunday breakfast in the kitchen of my apartment. Our knees touched as we sat at the fold-down table.

"Look, Nick, if you're going to weasel..."

"Have I ever weaseled on a promise to you?"

Maggie looked at the ceiling, lowered her gaze, and rolled her eyes as though she was about to faint. Later, after she'd "done her face" and put on a brown and orange dress that swirled away from her slender legs when she turned fast enough, we strolled hand in hand toward the Methodist Church three blocks away.

"Such a nice morning," Maggie said as we gazed at blue skies and a few fluffy clouds. A breeze tugged gently at her hair.

I walked her to the church, moseyed on to Kellog's Drug Store a couple of blocks down Division Street, bought a copy of the Sunday Chicago Times, and strolled back to the apartment.

I read about the Chicago Bears' dim prospects of winning a game. The cat, which had been content lying beside me on the couch, jumped down, went to the door, and rubbed against Maggie's leg when she entered the apartment.

She kicked off her shoes, slipped out of her panties, pulled the dress over her head, and went into the bedroom.

"Shame," I said. "You having just come from church and all."

"I'm sorry if I embarrassed you," she said.

"I missed you," I said as I lay in bed on my back beside her. "But you do wear me out."

"Ha. You recover fast enough."

I kissed her ear.

"I missed you too," she admitted. "But I enjoyed visiting my sons and their families."

That evening, after driving my Escort through the four blocks of downtown Central City, I turned on Park Drive. I entered the half-empty blacktop parking lot above a natural amphitheater in Oak Glen Park. Oak and elm trees rimmed the top of the west and north banks. A small lake is hemmed in on the east side. The bandstand nestled at the back of the hollow. It had been repaired some twenty years before but was still kept freshly painted. The park was one of Central City's "Points of Pride."

After I parked the car, Maggie and I strolled down a wide cement path past semicircular rows of wooden park benches.

She led me to the front row. Large speakers stood guard at either end of the stage. A path led away from the benches up to a concession stand. Behind the benches, a grassy slope provided space for blankets and lawn chairs.

I slouched on a park bench, hoping time wouldn't stand still as we waited for the concert to begin that late August evening. The afternoon heat had dissipated. A breeze rustled through the trees high above. Clouds, highlighted by slanting sun rays, drifted by now and then.

Maggie introduced me to Nina Fitch, or was it Fintch? They chatted about the public library and how Nina loved the books Maggie chose for her daughter. Nina's plump face was as lined as her wrinkled shorts. Her faded blouse was a size too small.

Her daughter, perhaps six years old, with straight brown hair and large brown eyes, squirmed her way onto my lap. She smelled of Ivory soap.

"Do you like me?" she said. Her eyes held mine until I said, "Sure."

She bounced a couple of times and said, "Bet you don't know my name."

Before I could admit my ignorance, she said, "When will the music start?"

I shrugged.

"Why don't you talk to me?"

And so it went. The questions came faster than I could answer. Eventually, I just said, "Because." She countered with, "Why?"

Nina and her daughter left to join a woman and two children a couple of rows behind us. I sighed and squirmed on the bench. Two old guys settled on the bench behind us. They argued about the proposal for a mega hog farm north of town that would, according to one, stink up the town and poison the water supply.

"That's all a bunch of bullshit," one of the guys said. "Modern technology prevents the smell and the pollution."

"It's not a bunch of bullshit, it's hog shit, and nothing is gonna keep it from smelling and polluting. Corporations don't care about modern technology. It costs money. The only thing they care about is profit, and to hell with the rest," the other voice replied.

I'd heard the arguments often. I tried to tune them out by observing the variety of humans flowing down the ramp. Musical instrument cases, large and small, were attached to some. Those people, all dressed in black slacks – white shirts for men, white blouses for women – meandered to behind the bandstand and eventually appeared on the stage.

Sounds, at first isolated, became a raucous chorus of discordant notes and challenged the boom of a kettle drum.

I said, "They aren't very good, are they?"

Maggie faced me.

"You know, smart ass, they're just tuning up. Sit up before you slide off the bench."

"Speaking of ass, you've got a built-in cushion to sit on. I'm all muscle."

She stood and looked behind us, as slim as a teenager. Well, almost. A brown belt surrounded the top of her tan shorts. A black, silky blouse fitted nicely over her breasts. Tan sandals completed the outfit. Her hair, near the color of her shorts, was cropped and gave her that cool look.

"People still sit on the slope on blankets," she said. "I used to do that with my boys. They never sat still. I spent more time trying to keep track of them than I did listening."

I stood to keep the disfigurement of my rear from becoming permanent. Familiar faces, some I could even connect with names, were scattered among the swelling crowd.

Richard Bowles, editor of the Central City Press, and his wife, Ruth, ambled down the walk as racing kids jostled them. Poor Richard. He'd told me once that he would have left Central City long ago if it hadn't been for his kids.

"What do the kids have to do with it?" I asked.

"They're so happy here. They like school, their friends; everything is so comfortable for the whole family."

I wondered then if I would have felt trapped in the gutless news coverage of the press if I had a family.

The tall frame of Luther Bishop stood out in a line at the refreshment stand near the top of the slope. He had been an unsuccessful candidate for state representative in the last election.

To the left of the stand, Bruce Locket sought souls for his *Church of the Gathering*. I turned away, hoping he wouldn't spot me and come seeking publicity. I waited a minute or so and looked back. He had moved on. But Big Ed Coburn, the county board chairman and farm implement dealer, was there glad-handing voters.

A steady stream of squealing children flowed back and forth in front of and behind Maggie and me. I sat and continued to squirm, trying to find a comfort zone.

Maggie said, "See, I told you we'd have to get here early for a good seat. The benches are nearly filled already."

More people filed down from the parking area and onto the benches or carried their lawn chairs and blankets to open spots on the slope.

"Yeah," I said. "Those latecomers will be sorry. They won't be able to hear a thing."

I smelled the whiskey and cigar before I was shoved against Maggie to make room on the bench for Big Ed.

"Surprised a hotshot like you would attend our little band concert," he said as he pressed his big ass against me. My inclination was to punch him in the nose. That's just what he wanted so he could file charges. He'd been harassing me ever since I cut him out of a photo that appeared in the Central City Press while I was working there.

Maggie glanced at Big Ed and turned away. She'd once said, "When that creep looks at me, I feel like he's looking up my skirt, and I'm not wearing any underwear."

We both tried to ignore him as the noise from the stage increased. The kettle drum guy, not much taller than the drum, thumped it with a drumstick, adjusted the tightness of the skin with turnbuckle-like things, and thumped it again. The band director appeared in a matching coat and pants and a generous portion of shoulder decorations. He stood facing the band. A single note sounded from one of the instruments. This apparently was a signal for the others to duplicate the sound.

Big Ed stood, sneered down at me, and waddled away.

The director tapped his baton on the podium. The noise from the stage ceased, and the murmur of conversation behind us dwindled. The conductor raised his baton.

A whip-cracking sound bit into the air. A scream followed. The director's baton remained frozen in the air. An instant of silence was shattered by, "Somebody help! She's bleeding! I think she's been shot!"

The screamer stood in the third row to our left, on the far side of the amphitheater. I dodged benches and people and raced to the scene. I put my hands on the screamer's shoulders and assured her it would be all right to rest her lungs. She collapsed and edged away from the body of a young woman sprawled on the bench. Blood dripped from the young woman's forehead.

I pressed a finger into her neck. No pulse. She was dead.

MURDER INHERITED - CHAPTER ONE

A J.B. Bancroft Mystery
By **MARTIE LITER OGBORN**

For years I repeatedly told Natasha I would never return. Yet here I am, freezing to death, locked in my own refrigerated trailer in Central City. When minding my own business, I should trust my feminine intuition. It is always better than my impulsive reactions.

Natasha and I have been friends since 5th grade in one of those friend-for-life friendships. So when she called me on Monday and sheepishly reminded me I owed her a favor, pleaded for my help, and asked if I would please come back to Central City, I impulsively told her I would be there in 48 hours. I was driving in her direction anyway, with a load of flowers scheduled for delivery in Springfield, Illinois, just an hour south.

My name is J.B. Bancroft. I am a transportation specialist. In other words, I am a truck driver.

After the flowers were unloaded at the warehouse Wednesday, my purple International semi and I rangled the empty reefer trailer north to the river side of Central City. I turned into Twinkler Trucking's parking lot.

I called from the cab of my truck and left a message on Natasha's answering machine. She had been a dispatcher for

Twinkler for the last five years and was recently promoted to Operations Manager. The message I left said I would rest a few hours in the bunk of my cab before I came to her office. I had driven through the night.

By 4:00p.m., Natasha's shift would be over. The plan was to have dinner and figure out where her fiancé, Zach, whom she had just hired as a driver for Twinkler Trucking, could have disappeared. He had already been out of communication for almost a week. Obviously, that was the way he wanted it, but why? In trucking, there is a truism: "YOU may know where you are, and GOD may know where you are, but if your DISPATCHER doesn't know where you are, YOU and GOD better be on good terms."

Before I crawled into the bunk behind the passenger seat of my cab, I pulled the curtains across the windshield. I wiggled out of my boots and jeans and reached over to lock the outside door, but the handle wasn't there. I'm sure I looked angry, half because the door was open and half because I was wearing only a shirt and underwear.

I wanted to yell, "What the fuck!" but seeing a shadow of a man standing off to the right, the words caught in my throat. I grabbed my thumper from the floor, a piece of wood like a billy club I used to check tire inflation. Before I could say anything or close the door, the thug reached into the bunk and grabbed my arm, dragging me to the ground. With no other choice, I rolled into a ball and made every effort to resist. I landed in a lump but kept my head from hitting the ground. The tire thumper ended up on the gravel in front of me. I stretched to retrieve the heavy baton when a large shoe stepped on my wrist. My eyes followed a pair of jeans up to the bastard's waist when a silver belt buckle in the shape of a semi flashed in the sunlight. His body odor was awful. Spicy and foul from overuse of aftershave and underuse of soap. He let out a disgusting guttural laugh, which stopped when I pounded my right fist on his left instep. He grabbed the tire thumper; it came down on my head.

I came to on a familiar frigid floor and realized I had been stuffed in my own reefer trailer. The smell of roses was still strong. I had been out cold, but for how long? The watch on my left wrist was smashed and had stopped at 1:02pm. Had my cab and trailer been moved? I could feel panic coming up from my gut. *Settle down.* I reassured myself. *You know there is a safety latch on the inside of the trailer.*

Barefooted, I quickly took a few steps on the bitter cold aluminum floor. I shoved on the trailer door safety latch and was confused when it didn't open; the trailer seemed to be up against something solid.

I felt sure the trailer was still connected to my cab because I had secured the trailer lock before climbing into the bunk. The trailer wasn't moving, but the reefer was running full blast, probably because I hadn't turned it off when I left Springfield. Hauling flowers requires a temperature of 33°, just above freezing, not like hauling watermelons or tomatoes. Produce needs a warmer setting, closer to 45°. Thinking about food, I was hungry, AND my body temperature was dropping.

After navigating to the back of the trailer, I found the stack of wooden pallets. With as much strength as I could muster, I slid the top pallet down to the floor. When it landed, there was a hollow ringing thud. There were no other sounds, nothing from the other side of the mobile ice box. I was starting to panic again; *how long could someone stay alive in this oversized coffin? Settle down and think.* I told myself.

The next pallet pulled off the top easier. Without my work gloves, my hands were pin cushions full of splinters. But I was mad... and throwing things helped. Who the HELL did he think he was, locking me in my own reefer?

I tried to make more noise. With a pivoting motion, I flung a pallet as hard as I could into the side of the trailer. I stopped to listen. There still was nothing to hear. Even if the jerk who put me in here was the only person who could hear me, I knew I had to find a way out.

The next pallet made a different noise. The sound gave me hope that a slat had come loose. With some effort, I now had a weapon in case whoever opened the door was the enemy. I hoped someone, anyone, would open the door!

I dragged a pallet to the end of the trailer, leaned it against the door, and banged the Morse code signal SOS. If anyone was nearby, I was sure they would notice, and I would be saved. Soon, I could no longer keep track of my code. Was that two or three short knocks?

Confused and getting sleepy, I was yielding to hypothermia. Now what? All I knew for sure was that I was running out of steam. When I was moving, I wasn't shivering, and my teeth weren't chattering. I had to sit down and rest even if I couldn't hear myself think over the noise of my teeth. On the stack of pallets, I pulled my arms under my shirt and drew my legs tight to my core. I could rest for a second.

ACKNOWLEDGEMENTS

-My companion, Arthur Oliveira, for supporting my efforts to fill the roles of publisher, author, and creative director of Bancroft Mysteries, LLC.
-My sister, Jeannie, for her lifetime encouragement.
-Friends Ginny, Carol, and Janet, for their willingness to read and reread manuscript drafts and for offering invaluable feedback.
-Jean Marie Stine, my mentor and original publisher of Bob Liter's books, for supporting my goal of becoming an independent publisher.
- Mom and Dad, Bob and Lillian Liter, for inspiring me to follow a path of passion and adventure, to celebrate their legacy and leave mine.
- My sons, Rob and Scott, and to their father, my late husband, Jerry, for believing in me.

With my Deepest Appreciation,
Martie Liter Ogborn

NOTE FROM THE PUBLISHER

Bancroft Mysteries, LLC was established in 2022, promotes mysteries written by Bob Liter, publishes romances authored by Bob Liter under the pen name Cyn Castle, and provides a platform to write and publish sequels to the Bancroft Mysteries series.

The entertaining manuscripts, written in and about the 1980s and 90s are as true to Bob's original work as possible to preserve that particular time and place in history while proving the reader with an enjoyable reading experience.

Reviews and recommendations are very important to an author and help contribute to a book's success. If you have enjoyed Love and Other Sports, please recommend it to your friends and colleagues. And please consider posting a review on Amazon or your preferred review site. Thank you.

BOOKS BY THIS AUTHOR

Murder By The Book

Nick Bancroft, a freelance reporter, inherits a rundown detective agency in Cental City and embarks on a new career. Date rape drugs are discovered at two murders, with sex etiquette books left at the scenes. Nick is hired by the first victim's father, Ramsey Sinclair, to find the killer. Mr. Sinclair unceremoniously dismisses Nick from the case when the police arrest a suspect.

Mr. Randolph, the suspect's attorney, hires Nick's AAA Detective Agency and a Chicago detective, Miss Faustine, to work "closely" with Bancroft. Bancroft's focus is interrupted when he begins a love affair with a receptionist, Maggie Atley, from a neighboring office.

Bancroft is banking on solving the murders and selling the story to the Chicago Times. As the case unfolds, there is enough danger, drama, and deception to fill a book. Nick finds that few things are as they seem. In his enthusiasm, he becomes the target of a shooter and also the target of charming Maggie Atley's affections.

August Is Murder

IN THIS "GRIPPING" MYSTERY THRILLER, NICK BANCROFT WILL PUT UP WITH JUST ABOUT ANYTHING!

A sexy nudist hires Nick Bancroft to defend her from threats on her life; Nick volunteers 24-hour protection. Now, he is the target, and August becomes even hotter when someone tries to burn him alive. Nick is not one to turn tail and run, especially with two murders and Lady Godiva to protect. Nick's true love, second only to the Cubs and bowling, Maggie Atley, is more than somewhat perturbed by the arrangement with his beautiful client.

After weeks of investigation, there are still unanswered questions. Who are the bad guys? What does a mysterious club have to do with the murders? Can Nick survive another losing season by his beloved Chicago Cubs? Is this the last inning for Nick and Maggie?

Death Sting

PRIVATE EYE NICK BANCROFT'S DEADLIEST CASE When Vicki Fowler's body is found covered with bee stings in a Central Illinois pasture, the sheriff calls her death an accident. Freelance reporter and private detective Nick Bancroft doesn't believe it. He learns the victim lived in a home for young unwed mothers who work as waitresses and whores at a local nightclub. Murder suspects include an alcoholic handyman, the man and wife who operate the home, a nightclub operator and his henchman, and a sheriff's deputy. Federal agents on the trail of an international porn ring try to halt Nick's investigation. Nick is beaten and thrown into a ditch. Later he and his earthy lover, Maggie Atley, are dumped in a deep lake with weights tied to their ankles. Nick Bancroft Mysteries are: "Power packed ... draw the reader into the story from the opening line and hold the attention to the surprising end. Peopled with fascinating, credible characters." Holly Martin in Black Dragon Reviews. "As action-packed as Tom Clancy's Jack Ryan without the military minutiae, and as filled with both local color and universal appeal as Carl Hiassen's gems." Bill Knight, Community Word.

"Deft tales of murder, complicity, and downright evil, gripping narratives which appeal to the lover of good action-packed mystery thrillers. Highly Recommended." Molly's Reviews.

Point Of Murder

Nick Bancroft, a freelance reporter and private detective, enjoys a mundane existence in Central City, operating a one-person detective agency. He supplements his pauper's income by selling news stories to the Chicago Times. In a small apartment, Nick and his roommate Maggie, share frivolous lovemaking and the responsibility of feeding a stray cat that adopted them. On the surface, it seems perfect.

The bed of roses ends abruptly when Nick's destitute young friend, Bobby Scalf, is found murdered with a blunt six-inch spike in his head. Nick becomes a suspect when a second murder victim is discovered in the abandoned building where the boy lives.

While Nick tries to find out who killed the boy, he uncovers corruption involving the town council, the school board, the police chief, and the local newspaper publisher. Nick survives several attempts on his life, and his lady's life is put at risk before Nick nails the killer and exposes the town's secrets. There may need to be more than solving the town's problems to solve the problems between Maggie and Nick. Is it really over?

And The Band Played On

Nick Bancroft, freelance reporter and private detective, enjoys a mundane existence in Central City, operating a one-man detective agency. He supplements his pauper's income by selling news stories to the Chicago Times. In a small apartment, Nick and his roommate Maggie, share frivolous lovemaking and the responsibility of feeding a stray cat that adopted them. On the surface, it seems perfect.

The bed of roses ends abruptly when Nick's destitute young friend, Bobby Scalf, is found murdered with a blunt six-inch spike in his head. Nick becomes a suspect when a second murder victim is discovered in the abandoned building where the boy lives.

While Nick tries to find out who killed the boy, he uncovers corruption involving the town council, the school board, the police chief, and the local newspaper publisher. Nick survives several attempts on his life, and his lady's life is put at risk before Nick nails the killer and exposes the town's secrets. Solving the town's problems may not be enough to solve the problems festering between Maggie and Nick. Is it really over?

ABOUT THE AUTHORS

Bob Liter (1923-2008), a Drake University graduate, earned his journalism degree in 1947. He began his career as a reporter, columnist, and copy editor. After he retired from the Peoria Journal Star, he wrote the Bancroft Mysteries in the early 2000s. He also wrote a series of contemporary romances from the 1980s under the pen name Cyn Castle.

Lillian Hyde Liter (1931-2008) married Bob Liter on March 4, 1950. Lillian is the inspiration for Maggie Atley in the Bancroft Mysteries, especially in the charming way she deals with the protagonist Nick Bancroft, a self-proclaimed "male chauvinist piggy," who resembles Bob Liter with his wit and bodaciously gutsy approach to life.

Martie Liter Ogborn is celebrating her parents' legacy and leaving her own by independently publishing and writing sequels to Bob Liter's manuscripts. Her latest project is to personify the pen name Cyn Castle created by her father. The re-released novels bring to life the sex and sizzle of the '80s. The Cyn Castle Romances and the Bancroft Mysteries are set south of Chicago along Route 66 in a decade filled with equal parts nostalgia, desire, and mystery.

Made in the USA
Middletown, DE
03 April 2025